HONOR

A BIG SKY NOVELLA

KRISTEN PROBY

AMPERSAND PUBLISHING, INC.

HONOR

A Big Sky Novella
By
Kristen Proby

HONOR

A Big Sky Novella - Heroes of Big Sky

Kristen Proby

Cover Design: By Hang Le

Published by Ampersand Publishing, Inc.

Paperback ISBN: 978-1-63350-074-7

PROLOGUE

~NICK~

"*I* haven't been released for duty."

The anger is swift. I want nothing more than to get back to work defending Her Royal Highness, Princess Nina. Protecting the royal family is important, and a joy.

I enjoy it—and them.

But since I was shot in the line of duty a month ago, ruining muscles in my right shoulder and chest, working has been impossible.

I'm coming out of my skin with boredom.

"Good," Nina says with a definitive nod. "I told you that it was too soon, Nick."

"It's been a bloody month," I mutter and shove my hand through my hair. "I need to resume my duties."

"You need to heal," Nina disagrees and props her hands on her hips. "I'm protected. I'm not saying we don't need you. But for now, I have protection, and I need you to get well."

"She's right." Nina's husband, Sebastian, says as he walks into the room. We've been in the couple's Montana home for several months now; since before *the incident* happened.

Neither Nina nor Sebastian has been in a hurry to return to London.

"Sir, I feel fine. I've begun to work out again, building up the muscles in my shoulder."

"And you reinjured yourself," Sebastian says, raising a brow. "Yes, your doctor called me."

"So much for patient confidentiality."

"You shouldn't have listed me as your emergency contact," Sebastian says with a nod.

"I don't remember doing that," I reply, narrowing my eyes.

"Well, you were unconscious when I filled out the paperwork," he says, waving me off. "Your health is the most important thing. My *wife*, the most precious person in my life, is your job. Of course, I want you at one hundred percent before we reinstate you."

"Of course." I know that arguing with the prince is futile. I've worked for the royal family for several years.

"I know being idle isn't in your nature," Nina says. Not only is she my charge, but she's also become my friend over the past two years. I like her very much. This family has become closer to me than *mine*. "And you have to be bored out of your mind."

"Understatement."

"But it won't be forever. You're going to heal, and you'll be back on your feet in no time."

"It's not my feet that bother me."

No, it's this motherfucking shoulder that still sings like a bitch every time I move.

"I know you can do this," Nina continues. "But to make sure, I have some new requirements."

I raise a brow and wait as she continues.

"You'll be moving out of the security headquarters."

I frown. I have to leave the property? Since I came to work for the princess, I've been living out in the guesthouse, where our headquarters is located. "I live there. Where am I supposed to go?"

"It's too tempting to work out with the other guys out there," she says. "You're moving into my old lake house just down the street. There's not a barbell in sight down there. It's been empty for a couple of months. Someone should use it. It's secluded and quiet —the perfect place to rest."

Or the perfect place to rehab alone, where no one can watch me like a hawk and tell me to stop.

"And, to make sure you rest, I've hired you a nurse."

I blink at her and then scowl. "You hired me a *babysitter?*"

"Call it what you want, but a medical professional will be living with you, twenty-four hours a day until you've healed and have been given permission to return to work."

"So, I'm being punished."

Nina laughs and shakes her head. "Nick, you get to live in a nice house on the lake. It's snowy and peaceful, not to mention, ridiculously beautiful. Why are you complaining? Take the time to rest. Catch up on some reading. Binge some Netflix. Let yourself heal. Jordan is an excellent nurse and comes highly recommended. So, you'll be in good hands.

"You almost *died* protecting me and my family, Nick. If you think I'm going to sit by and watch you continue to injure yourself, all because you're too stubborn for your own good, you're sorely mistaken."

I turn to Sebastian, but he just nods in agreement with his wife.

"She's right. You're a valuable member of our team, and I need you at one hundred percent. Take the time to recover, Nick. We'll be here when you're ready."

"A bloody babysitter," I mutter as I turn toward the door that leads down to headquarters. If this dude, this *nurse*, thinks he can hold me back from rehabbing and returning to work, he'll get a lesson in who the boss is real quick. "I'll be at your place this afternoon."

"You're going to love it," Nina calls after me. "I promise!"

CHAPTER 1

~JORDAN~

The snow is fresh.

After living in Phoenix for more than five years, I missed this the most: the snow. The change of seasons. Don't get me wrong, being able to swim in the complex pool over Thanksgiving weekend is fun, but I'm a Montana girl through and through.

I missed big, bulky sweaters, hot drinks, and burrowing under blankets. I could do that in Arizona, but I had to crank the A/C to give the illusion of winter.

That's not a problem here in Cunningham Falls, Montana.

I grew up here. My roots run deep. And I guess, way down, I always figured I'd be back.

I just didn't plan on not having a job when I did.

I follow the GPS and turn my Toyota into the

driveway of a house on Whitetail lake, then cut the engine and take a deep breath.

I'm a registered nurse. I worked my ass off to get through school, and I love what I do. But there are no available jobs right now, and I need work. So when my cousin told me her friend was looking for a caretaker for a few weeks, I inquired.

I'm ridiculously overqualified for this.

But it's a job.

Not to mention, I'll be staying in this killer house on the lake for a while, which means I won't have to live with my mother.

I love her, but she gets on my last nerve.

I take one last deep breath, then get out of the car and retrieve my suitcase from the back seat, carrying it up the steps to the front door.

I ring the bell and wait. When there's no answer, I ring it again and turn to admire the evergreen trees, heavy with snow. It's like something out of a painting.

The door swings open behind me, and I turn. Then stop cold.

Holy crap.

This guy is my patient?

"Hi, I'm Jordan," I say, holding out my hand to shake.

He looks at my hand and then back up at my face. He's wearing dark-rimmed glasses, and his blue eyes behind the lenses narrow. His brown hair is messy as if he's been running his hands through it all day.

He's tall and broad. Lean. Certainly healthy.

"You're a girl," he says.

"A woman," I confirm, wondering if he has brain damage. "Thanks for noticing."

"I was expecting a man," he says and still doesn't let me through the door.

"Why?"

He doesn't reply, just leans against the doorjamb and watches me.

"Because my name is Jordan?" He lifts a brow. "Yeah, I get that a lot, but it's really unisex. My dad wanted a boy and named me Jordan. Would have named a male child that, too, actually. Are we going to stand in the doorway all day? If so, I'll grab a scarf out of my car."

He doesn't say a word, just walks into the house. I follow him after I wrestle my suitcase over the threshold.

"This is a really nice place," I say as I close the door behind me and slip out of my coat, hanging it on a hook. I toe off my boots and follow Nick into the kitchen—at least I assume this is Nick. I mean, who else would it be? "Should we talk?"

"What would you like to talk about?" he asks as he pours cream into a mug full of coffee and turns to me, sipping the hot beverage.

Okay, so he's a bit rude and not hospitable at all.

I've worked with worse.

Hell, I've *lived* with worse.

And I have to admit, that accent gives me little shivers.

"We should probably go over what you need and want, and I can tell you what orders I've been given. You know, start with the basics."

"I don't want or need anything."

I nod and boost myself up onto a stool at the kitchen island. I'm short. I'm always boosting myself up somewhere.

"Nina did tell me that you might not be super excited to have me here."

"Don't you have somewhere else to be? The hospital? A clinic?"

"Nope." My voice is cheerful as I spin on the stool and offer him my brightest smile. "I've recently moved home from Arizona, and I'm between jobs. So, this works out great. I mean, it's not good that you're injured, but—"

"I get it."

"Anyway, I'm all yours for the foreseeable future." His jaw firms, making me laugh. "Oh, come on. Don't be so excited. I'm a likeable gal. Pretty agreeable. I'm an excellent conversationalist. And I can cook like crazy. Seriously, Rachel Ray has nothing on me. Or that Pioneer Woman. Have you seen the dimples on her? She's just so *pretty*. And she can cook. I mean, is that fair?"

Nick pinches the bridge of his nose.

"Do you ever *not* talk?"

I slump on the stool. "Huh? Sure. I mean, if you don't want to talk, that's okay. I'll just fill you in on what I know, and we can go from there. Nina wants me to cook and clean, and make sure you're not overdoing it with your shoulder. If you have questions or concerns about your injury, I can take a look. You're not supposed to go crazy with exercise, at least not for a little while yet."

"I'm a grown-ass man, and I'll do whatever the bloody hell I want with my shoulder."

"Sure." I nod and rummage around in my purse for my lip moisturizer. "I mean, you're right. You can. Except your job is important, and if you don't follow the rules, you can't go back to work. Aha! There it is." I pull out the tube and rub it on my lips before tossing it back into my bag and smiling at the surly Nick. "What do you want for dinner? I figure we can do takeout tonight, and then I'll go to the grocery and stock up on some things later."

"I don't care." He sighs and sets his empty mug in the sink. "Whatever you want."

"Italian it is. I haven't had Ciao since I got home, and I'm totally craving it. What room do you want me to take?"

His eyes narrow on me again.

"You're staying here?"

"Twenty-four-seven," I confirm. "And don't look so scared. I won't be in your way. I have stuff to do."

"Jesus," he mutters and pushes his hand through his

already messy hair. "I'm in the master. You can take any of the others."

"Okay." I hop off the stool and return to the foyer to retrieve my suitcase. "I'll just go get this settled, and then I'll order dinner."

He nods, and I wrestle my case upstairs, taking the bedroom farthest from the master. We're both going to want our privacy.

If there was a bedroom on the first floor, I'd have taken that. But we'll make do.

The house is smaller than I imagined, but it's beautiful. All the rooms face the lake, and they each have huge windows so you're sure not to miss the views.

Now that I think about it, this would be my dream house—something on the small side with an incredible view. It just doesn't get any better than this.

I unpack my suitcase and store it in the closet. When everything is in its place and organized, I freshen my blond hair, slick more moisturizer on my lips, and skip down the steps. A quick search tells me that Nick is sitting in the living room, reading something on his tablet.

"All moved in," I announce.

He grunts.

"Do you know what you want for dinner?"

"Just get two of whatever you want."

I frown and sit on a chair across from him. "I'm getting all the carbs in the world. You don't strike me as a carb guy."

"Why not?"

"Well." I look him over and feel myself start to salivate. "I mean, you're lean and muscly. And I'm not flirting." I shake my head. "I'm just stating a fact as a medical professional that you don't look like you eat many carbs. In my professional opinion. Professionally."

"So, you're being professional, then." For the first time since I got here, I see humor in his blue eyes, and it gives me hope that I won't be living with Scrooge for this entire assignment.

"Completely. So, are you sure you want what I'm having?"

"Add a salad on the side," he says and looks back down at the screen.

"Okay, but I warned you. I'll order and go pick it up. Shouldn't take long."

He nods, and I leave the room to do just that.

By the time I'm driving into town to fetch the food, I've relaxed quite a bit. Nick might have a bark to him, but he'll loosen up. He can't be grouchy *all* the time.

Darkness has fallen, but the moon is high, reflecting off of the fresh snow. It's just past Thanksgiving, so the town has already hung holiday lights and décor throughout the downtown area, making it look like the set of a Hallmark movie.

I freaking love it.

I don't have to wait for the food, and when I get back to the house, I dish it onto plates, grab utensils and napkins, and deliver the meal to Nick, who's still in the living room.

He did turn on the gas fireplace while I was gone, making the room cozy.

"Thanks," he says and then raises a brow at me. "You weren't kidding."

"Bread, pasta, rich sauce. You're welcome. But I did get your salad."

"How do you eat like this and stay so little?" he asks before taking a bite of his bread.

"Wait. Are we having a *conversation*?"

He chews, silently waiting for me to reply.

"I'm blessed with a crazy fast metabolism," I reply with a shrug and moan in delight when the first bite hits my tongue. "Jesus God, that's good. Mmm. I mean, I remember what it tastes like, but it's so much better than my memories."

I shovel more in and sigh in happiness.

"Oh, I also run for exercise," I say, dabbing my lips. "So, luckily, I can eat pretty much whatever I want, and things don't get too out of hand. How's yours?"

"What? Oh, it's fine."

"Nick. Come on, it's better than fine."

"Okay, it's pretty damn good."

I nod in satisfaction. "Have you had their Italian nachos? We have to get them next time. I can't believe I forgot them."

"I'm going to gain fifty pounds," he mumbles.

"Nah, we'll just eat like this once a week. As a treat.

12

I'm all about healthy meals the rest of the time, I promise. Except I have one very firm rule. And I will not bend it."

"I can't wait to hear this," he says, his voice heavily laced with sarcasm.

"If I make tacos, and I *will* make tacos, we have margaritas with said meal. That is not up for discussion."

His lips twitch. I almost got a smile out of him!

"I can live with that."

"Good." I set my empty plate aside. "I'll make a grocery list tonight and leave it on the counter. Just add whatever you want to it."

"I'll go to the store with you."

"That's fine, too." I sit back and pull my sock-clad feet up under me. "Oh my God, I'm full of carbs, and this fire is amazing. I could fall asleep."

"Don't. I can't carry you upstairs."

I smile at him. "Don't worry. I won't. Although, I've always been able to sleep anywhere. The car, the plane, the floor."

"Not me," he says. Just when I think he's going to say more, he picks up his tablet and turns it back on.

I guess we won't be chatting it up late into the night. Nick's a man of few words, that's for sure. I wonder if that's with everyone, or just me.

Without another word, I carry our dirty dishes into the kitchen. I clean up, store the leftovers in the fridge, and start the dishwasher.

Then, I take the magnetic to-do pad off the fridge and start making my grocery list. I search the contents of the kitchen and discover that I'm pretty much starting from scratch.

Which is actually kind of fun. I'm sure I'll forget something, but luckily, the store isn't far away.

I shoot Nina a text, letting her know that I'll be breaking the bank on groceries tomorrow. The fact that I have a princess's phone number is still a foreign concept to me.

The whole situation is nuts.

But I'm home, and I have a job. That's really all that matters.

CHAPTER 2

~NICK~

"I won't eat that." I take the sugary strawberry jam out of the cart and put it back on the shelf.

"Good, more for me." Jordan smiles sweetly and retrieves the jam, putting it back in the basket. "I like it on my English muffins in the morning."

"You have quite the sweet tooth."

"Yeah, it's a good thing I run about five miles a day."

She pushes the cart, and I follow a few steps behind, doing my best not to stare at her firm, tight ass.

Okay, I'm not doing my *best*. I've looked at least four times already. Jordan's not the male nurse I was expecting. Instead, she's this compact, gorgeous little ray of sunshine, with her golden blond hair and bright smile. Not to mention, her green eyes would likely stop traffic in Times Square. If it were anyone else, her optimistic happiness would get on my bloody nerves.

But so far, all she's done is lighten my mood, which is unexpected, to say the least. I was ready to throw her out on her ass yesterday.

And today, I want to throw her out for completely different reasons.

Because keeping my hands to myself is going to be a test of wills that I'm not sure I can win.

Maybe it's been too long since I last got laid.

I think back over the previous year, trying to remember when it was. If I'm not mistaken, it wasn't in the last year at all.

That's fucking pathetic.

"Nick?"

"What?"

"Corn or flour?" Jordan holds up some taco shells. "Which one do you prefer?"

"Corn."

She throws both packages of shells into the cart.

"If you were going to buy both, why did you ask?"

"Because if you'd said flour, I would have only bought one."

She tosses her scarf over her shoulder with a sassy flip and turns out of the aisle, running straight into another cart.

"Oh, crap!" she exclaims. Then, to my amazement, she squeals and runs to the other woman to hug her tightly. "Oh my gosh, it's so good to see you!"

"I didn't know you were back," the brunette says as she pulls away. "Are you here with Jeremy?"

"No," Jordan says immediately, shaking her head. "Fresh start."

"Ah, gotcha." The other woman turns to me with a curious smile. "Hi. I'm Sidney."

"Sorry," Jordan says and gestures to me. "This is Nick. He's a...friend. Nick, this is my cousin, Sidney."

"Nice to meet you," I reply with a nod.

"Let's get together before Christmas," Sidney says to Jordan. "You can fill me in on things."

"Sounds great. I'll text you."

They hug once more, and then we're off again, Jordan filling the basket with more food than I'll likely eat in a month.

"So, do you have a lot of family here?" I ask her as she chooses a box of oatmeal and tosses it into the basket.

"Yeah. My family goes back a long ways. I'm related to a lot of people. Lots of cousins. And I know almost everyone."

"Why didn't you tell her I'm your patient?"

"Because, technically, you're not *my* patient. And because your medical situation is your business. It's not my place to say anything. Besides, you *are* my friend. I mean, not like a close one, but we're friendly."

She leads me down a seasonal aisle, and her face lights up. "Oh, this is fun. We'll pick up some Christmas stuff today, but I'll get the majority of my things later. I'll hit the thrift shop, too, because people change their décor all the time, and you can find some really great stuff there."

"Why are you buying holiday rubbish?"

She turns to me with a frown, her lips plump and glossy from that stuff she constantly spreads over them. Fucking hell, I want to kiss her.

"Because it's December. Which means it's almost Christmas. Don't you like having holiday things in the house?"

"It's not on my radar, no."

"You're telling me the royal family doesn't decorate for the holidays?"

"Of course, they do. Or their staff does, at least. It's my job to protect them, not hang stockings."

She tosses red and green baking sprinkles into the cart, making me frown.

"But don't you see your family?"

"No."

"Why?"

"I just don't." I exhale and push my hand through my hair. I'm not getting into this. Especially in the Christmas aisle of the grocery store. "There's no need to go to all that trouble."

"Oh, it's no trouble."

"It's not my house to decorate," I remind her, but she just shrugs one shoulder.

"I already talked to Nina about it. She's fine with me making the place look a little festive. Don't worry, I won't go overboard. Gosh, speaking of Nina, I sure do like her. She's *so nice.*"

"How do you know her?" I ask. I know of everyone the princess has contact with, but Jordan's name has never been on that list.

"Oh, I don't. Not really. I met her through my other cousin, Willa. Well, she's not *technically* my cousin, but our families are close, so we've always said *cousin.* Willa told me that Nina needed someone for this job and put me in touch with her. I'm *so* glad she did."

There's that sweet smile again as we leave that aisle and turn down the coffee one. "We're going to need more coffee. And creamer. Sometimes, I like whipped cream in my coffee, so I'll grab that, too. I'm going to make strawberry pie over the weekend. That'll go well with the whipped cream, too."

"I thought we were going to be eating healthy."

She just laughs at my snide comment and leads me through the store. She stops to chat with those she knows, which seems to be almost everyone.

Once we're at the checkout, and the cashier gives us the amount due, I raise my eyebrows in surprise.

"We went a little crazy," I say as I reach for my wallet.

"There is literally *nothing* in that house," Jordan says, waving me off and pulling a card out of her wallet. "And this is taken care of."

I don't question her here, but the urge is strong.

Who the hell is taking care of it? I don't want Nina and Sebastian to pay for my bloody groceries.

That's above and beyond.

When we get to the car, I start to unload the groceries, but Jordan puts up a hand. Her face has gone from happy-go-lucky to all-business.

"No. These bags are heavy, and you will not lift them. I'm perfectly capable."

I don't say a word, just push her aside and resume grabbing the bags. Suddenly, she's in my way, all five-foot-nothing of her in my face.

"Nick, don't make me get mean."

Her voice is stern. Her face is hard.

Buggering hell, if I thought I was turned on by her earlier, that was nothing compared to this.

"Fine."

I get into the car and seethe as she handles all of the bags, then rolls the cart to the return slot behind us.

"It's gonna snow tonight," she says when she gets into the vehicle. She pulls her seatbelt on and starts the engine. "I'm so excited. I *love* the snow. Maybe I'll sit outside in it later. It's not too cold."

I don't answer. I don't like feeling incapable. Inadequate.

For fuck's sake, I should be working, not fetching groceries.

"I'm making the tacos for dinner. With margaritas."

"Whatever's your cup of tea."

She glances my way. "What crawled up your butt?"

I'm silent as she drives through town.

"Are you pissed because I didn't let you help with the bags? Nick, this is the whole reason I'm here. To make sure you *don't* do things like that. It's the whole point."

"Yeah, well, I don't have to like it."

"The less you do now, the faster you can get back to normal," she says. She sounds perfectly reasonable.

I still don't like it.

"Who's Jeremy?"

She doesn't miss a beat as she flips on her turn signal and then heads toward the lake house.

She also doesn't answer me.

"Jordan."

She clears her throat.

"You can tell me to mind my own business."

"It's not that. I'm trying to find a diplomatic way to answer that question. Jeremy is my ex-boyfriend."

"What's the non-diplomatic answer?"

"He's the piece of shit I stayed with for way too long."

I nod thoughtfully. "I like the second answer better."

"Me, too." She laughs and pulls into the driveway. "We dated through high school. I followed him to Arizona because that's where he wanted to go to college. And now, I'm home."

There is clearly a massive amount of information that she glossed over, but I figure I'll let it be for now.

Later, I'll run a search on this Jeremy. Shouldn't be difficult.

"I have a meeting at HQ this afternoon," I inform her. "I'll be gone for a couple of hours."

"Great, I'll go to the gym and get some miles in," she replies. I'd almost rather go to the gym with her and watch her run.

Of course, I know she wouldn't allow it.

"We're staying through the first of the year," Sebastian says. We're in HQ, holding our weekly briefing with both me and Randall Hunt, Sebastian's new head of security for both him and the Montana property. Sebastian has another security point man whenever he's in London.

I'm always assigned to Nina, no matter where she is in the world.

We also have other property detail men here.

"Why are you staying so long?" I ask, surprising His Highness.

"Nina would like to spend the holiday with her brother, and I have no objection to that."

I suspect that she wants to stay and supervise my recovery, but I keep that observation to myself. Things have been quiet here at the Montana property since *the incident* just a month ago, making life much easier for the security detail. But being on high alert, no matter the circumstances, is part of the job.

We finish going through some information, and just when Sebastian starts putting his coat on, he nods at me. "Nick, walk to the house with me?"

"Yes, sir."

We step out into the cold, calm air and climb the recently shoveled walk up to the main house.

"How are things going?" he asks.

I know he's asking about Jordan.

"It would be great if you could get me out of this."

He laughs and opens the door for me.

"My wife has her mind made up, I'm afraid. Is the nurse incompetent? Do you want us to find someone else?"

"That's not it." I shake my head in frustration. Maintaining my professionalism has never been a problem for me. And I'll be damned if I'll let it be an issue now. "I'm not used to having a babysitter."

We climb the stairs and find Nina sitting in the living room with her sister-in-law, Jenna.

"Your Highness." I bow my head.

"Hello, Nick. How nice to see you. How are things with Jordan?"

Sebastian laughs as he fetches himself a drink from the kitchen.

"What does that mean?" Nina demands, standing.

"She's fine," I reply, shaking my head.

"It means something," she insists, narrowing her eyes at me. "Do you hate her?"

"No." *No, I like her too much.* "She's fine, like I said."

"I've met Jordan before," Jenna says. "She's super sweet. A little young, but the nicest girl. I can't imagine she'll give you any trouble."

"She's a ray of sunshine," I mutter, remembering my assessment from earlier. "Just delightful."

"Are you being grumpy with her?"

Sebastian laughs again, making me scowl. "I'm always a little grumpy."

"Well, don't chase her off. Be nice."

"I'm perfectly nice."

"What does she look like?" Sebastian asks, earning a glare from me. "That bad?"

"No," Jenna says thoughtfully as a smile spreads over her face. "I think it's that *good.*"

"I'm leaving."

I march to the front door and fling it open to the sound of the three of them laughing behind me.

"Have a good evening," Nina calls out to me. I don't answer as I slam the door shut.

CHAPTER 3

~JORDAN~

*S*hawn Mendes sings in my ear as my feet pound the treadmill belt. I jog at my normal pace, watching Nick in the weight area below. We haven't been here for long, but I'm a mile into my run. He's been working out long enough to shed his sweatshirt, exposing the impressive muscles I've suspected all along were there.

I love winter, but it means more clothes, and Nick is impressive. I know he's lost some muscle mass since his injury just over a month ago, but he's still something to write home about.

Lord have mercy.

Now that the wound is fully healed, he's been cleared to start training with a professional. He's working with a trainer today, which put my mind at ease. So far, they've focused mostly on the lower body, but I can see the trainer—Todd, I believe his name is—

point at the free weights and tell Nick something. They nod and talk some more before Todd runs Nick through some exercises using very light weights.

I can see the strain and the frustration on Nick's handsome face, and my heart goes out to him. I don't know him well, but after a couple of days with him, I know he's not the type of person to remain idle. And I don't blame him, because I'm the same way.

But he has to go about healing the correct way, or this injury could follow him for the rest of his life.

Just as I cross the four-mile mark, Nick and Todd begin wrapping up their session. I slow to a walk and watch as Nick shakes Todd's hand, then glances up at me and nods before walking into the locker room.

I think that means he's done. Which is great timing.

I clean off my machine and walk down to the women's locker room to change. I'll shower at the house later. I don't like using public facilities.

It's a quirk. I have a few of those.

I do, however, quickly change into my street clothes and carry my duffle bag out of the locker room. I don't see Nick. I must have beat him out.

I take a seat on the bench between the two locker rooms and check my phone. I have a text from Sidney.

Sidney: *Let's have drinks on Friday! I need the 411 on what happened with J.*

I chuckle to myself as I type my reply.

Me: *I would love to, but I have a 24/7 job right now. Raincheck?*

"Hey."

I glance up and feel my eyes go wide at the sight of Jeremy standing in front of me. I stand and tuck my phone into my pocket.

"What's up?" I ask. I don't want to sound too welcoming, but I'm not a jerk, either.

"It's good to see you," he says and reaches for my hand, but I duck out of his way. "Listen, I've been meaning to talk to you…"

"Are you ready?"

Nick slides up next to me and, to my utter surprise, wraps his arm around my waist and smiles down at me.

He's smiling.

That doesn't happen often.

"Yes," I reply with a nod. "We'd better go."

"I was talking to you," Jeremy says, but Nick leads me away.

"And now you're not," he says over his shoulder as he escorts me out of the gym to my car. I fasten my seat belt and pull out of the parking lot, headed toward the lake house. Nick doesn't ask me about Jeremy at all.

"How was your workout?" I ask him.

"Tough," he replies and stares out the passenger window. "I knew I could lose a lot of strength in a month, but this is ridiculous."

"You didn't just stop working out," I remind him. "You were injured. But you'll be back to where you were in no time."

He nods. Before long, we're back at the house.

We both go our separate ways. I immediately jump in the shower to wash away the sweat from my run. Rather than blow-dry my hair, I twist it into a knot on my head, and with fresh lounge clothes on, head down to make dinner.

Tonight is going to be grilled salmon and asparagus with a Caesar salad.

I've just pulled the fish out of the fridge when Nick walks into the kitchen, also fresh from a shower. His dark hair is still wet, and a single droplet of water sits on his neck.

It's like it's begging me to lick it off.

I take a deep breath and open the fridge again, looking for the wine. I need a glass if Nick's going to be this close to me. Because holy hell in a handbasket, the man does things to me.

Sexy things.

And he's a patient—even though I told him he wasn't—so that's a no-go.

I pour the white wine into a glass, take a sip, and then smile at him.

"We're having salmon tonight. If that's okay."

"It's okay with me. I'm starving," he says.

"Working out will do that to you." I pull real butter out of the fridge, along with fresh herbs, and then go hunting for a cutting board.

"So, was that bloke Jeremy?" he asks and sits on the same stool I took the first day I was here.

"Yeah." I sigh and dump the butter into a bowl, getting it ready to mix with the garlic and herbs. "I didn't realize he was in Cunningham Falls. Not that I care."

I cut some chives and rosemary and keep chatting away.

"You know, it's interesting. You can be with someone for *years*, and when it's over, and you see them again, you can have absolutely no emotions about it." I look up at Nick with a frown. "Does that make me weird?"

Before he can answer, I shake my head and go back to chopping.

"Anyway, I told you that I followed him to Arizona. We went to college and lived together. Over time, things just got…different. You know? Like, he didn't like it when I spent time with my nursing school friends. And he thought I should quit college and go to work, and then after he was done with university, he'd work, and I could finish.

"But I was like, *no way.* I'm finishing my nursing degree. And I'm glad I did. He just wasn't meant for me. And, finally, a few months ago, I sat him down and told him it was over. Said I wanted to break up."

I mix the butter and herbs and then reach for the salmon and coat it with the mixture.

"He didn't take it well. Ended up hitting me."

"What the fuck?"

I glance up in surprise and feel my eyes widen at the

look of absolute horror and the promise of violence on Nick's face.

"Don't freak out," I say and turn my attention to the asparagus. "I called the cops, and he was arrested. I'm not the kind of girl to drop charges. I put up with a lot of crap from Jeremy over the years, but that was the end for me. So, while he sat in jail and figured that out, I packed my stuff and moved home."

"Good for you."

"Yeah. It was good for me. I didn't realize how much I'd missed Montana until I was here about a week, and the leaves had turned and crunched under my feet. That doesn't happen in Arizona. I missed the change of seasons."

"Maybe I shouldn't have interfered today," Nick says as he watches me prepare the food. "But you looked uncomfortable, and I didn't like the looks of him."

"It's fine. I'm not scared of him, but I'm also not eager to chat with him, you know?"

He laughs and nods his head, and I can't look away from him.

"You're seriously beautiful when you laugh."

His face sobers, and he blinks at me.

"Sorry. So, anyway, now you're up-to-date. Jeremy Dunnigan is solidly in my past. And now, for the present, I'm going to cook up these amazing pieces of salmon and—"

Suddenly, Nick turns me to him and lowers his

mouth to mine. The kiss starts in a frenzy, but after a few moments of our lips being fused, he lightens his grip and sort of sinks into me. It's like how they do it in the old movies, where it looks as if the guy might *die* if he doesn't kiss the girl.

I don't think I've ever been kissed like this before.

Nick's hands roam from my shoulders up to my face, and with the lightest touch, he frames my jawline and kisses me lightly yet thoroughly.

When he pulls back, his blue eyes are bright and pinned to mine.

"That's the only way I could get you to stop talking."

"Well." I swallow. "I guess it worked. Of course, it can't happen again."

His hands drop from my face down to my hands, and then he lets go and steps back.

"Why not?"

"You're my client."

A half-smile tickles his lips.

"*Nina* hired you, Jordan. Not me. If I had my way, I'd fire you and keep kissing you."

I bite my bottom lip at the thought, and his eyes shoot down to my mouth.

"You're not helping things," he growls.

"I really need this job," I say and frown at the asparagus.

"No one is saying you have to leave it," he replies. "But if it makes you feel better, I'll keep my hands to myself."

Well, no, that doesn't make me feel better. Because he's freaking *hot,* and that was maybe the best kiss of my entire life.

"Is that what you want?"

"I think, for right this minute, I want to cook dinner," I say slowly and glance up at him. His face has relaxed, and his eyes are warm as they watch me. "Because I'm hungry. Then, we'll take it from there."

"Fair enough." He turns to walk away but then stops short. He looks back at me. "You're safe with me, Jordan. I wouldn't do anything to jeopardize you or your job."

"Thanks." I smile and watch as he walks out of the room.

What in the hell do I think I'm doing? I take a big sip of my wine and then fan my face. Nick leaves quite the trail of heat when he exits a room.

Of course, it's nothing compared to the inferno he ignites when he's *in* the room.

I've never thought of having an affair with a patient or client before. Of course, if I worked for the hospital or were under contract, that would be against the rules.

But I'm not under contract. And like Nick said, I don't work for him. I work for Nina. And even if I do kiss him once in a while, I'm still capable of doing my job.

I push the fish and asparagus into the oven and then take a deep breath.

The truth is, I didn't want him to stop kissing me.

And when he laughed, I thought I might melt into a puddle right on the kitchen floor.

So, maybe I'll just see where this goes. Perhaps it'll go nowhere. Maybe the chemistry won't be there, and we'll go back to the way things were.

And perhaps pigs will fly through the window and do the cha-cha on the dining room table.

I smirk and finish my wine, then pour another glass.

Who knew that moving home would prove so *interesting*?

CHAPTER 4

~NICK~

"We turned a member of the press away from the gate yesterday," Aaron, one of the property's security men, says. We're about to wrap up our daily meeting at HQ.

"Was he paparazzi?" I ask.

"He said he was from a newspaper in Missoula," Aaron replies, shaking his head. "But who knows for sure? I sent him on his way, of course."

"Is anything else going on?" I ask.

"Princess Ellie and Liam arrive this afternoon," Randall says. "We'll have a full house again until after the holidays."

"Nina's excited," Sebastian says with a smile. "And Liam will most likely want to confer with you. Taking the security guard out of the man isn't an easy task."

"I've already been in touch with him," I add. "In fact, he's coming down to the lake house for pizza and football this evening. Any of you are welcome to join us."

The other men nod, and before long, we're wrapping up the meeting, and it's time for me to go back to the lake house.

It's not that Nina's old place isn't nice or comfortable. But it's not HQ. My quarters in the former guest house on the royal property are in what used to be the master bedroom. It's large enough to consider it a studio apartment. I prefer to be onsite, to be at the ready if anything should happen.

And I know that I'll get back here—hopefully, sooner rather than later. But damn if it doesn't put me in a shitty mood every time I have to leave and go back to the lake house. Because as sweet and sexy as Jordan is, I should be *working*.

I pull into the driveway and walk into the house. My eyebrows climb at the blaring sound of Mariah Carey's rendition of *All I Want for Christmas is You.*

I find Jordan in the living room, singing into the head of a nutcracker as if it's a microphone.

Her voice, or what I can hear of it over what's blasting through the speakers, isn't great. But she's confident.

I lean my good shoulder against the doorjamb and watch with amusement as Jordan begins the choreography part of her show, pointing to the tree she added in the corner. It's lit with small, white lights, and is about half full of ornaments.

It appears that today is the day Jordan's decided to decorate the house.

She does a quick spin and, with the flick of a wrist, hangs a gold ornament on the tree, then turns and sees me.

She doesn't flush. She doesn't look embarrassed or unsure of herself.

No, she freaking throws her head back and *laughs*. It's the sexiest damn sound I've heard in my life.

She picks up her phone and taps the screen, and the music quiets.

"Sorry, I didn't see you come in. What do you think?"

I stare at the tree, wishing she hadn't seen me. I would have liked to keep watching the free concert.

"Why did you put up a tree?"

"We went over this the other day at the store," she says and fusses with an ornament already on a branch, moving it to another location. Why? I have no idea. It looked just fine where it was. "It's December, Nick. Or should I call you Ebenezer?"

"It's a waste of time," I reply. "We'll be out of here before Christmas, so what's the point?"

"You *hope* you'll be out of here by Christmas," she says, but there's no tension in her voice. "And, in the meantime, it's the holidays. And *I* like the holidays, and I have to live here, too."

"Suit yourself."

"What's wrong with you?" she demands, her

patience seemingly gone as she sets a box of ornaments down. She props her hands on her hips and
scowls at me. "You're always *so* unhappy. I get it, you're
pissed that you can't work, but you were injured while
doing that job. And it's not like you're out on the
streets while you heal up. You're in a gorgeous house,
and you have freaking *royalty* looking out for you. I
mean, it's not ideal, but it doesn't suck *that* bad. So,
stop sulking. And stop being so damn *grumpy* all the
time."

I glare at her, irritated mostly because she's not
wrong.

I'm being a wanker.

And she doesn't deserve it.

I sigh and push my hand through my hair. I need a
bloody haircut.

"You're right." I glance at the tree and admit that it
looks nice in the corner where the windows meet. "I'm
a moody jerk since this all happened. It's not your
fault."

"Apology accepted." She grins and goes back to the
task at hand.

Just like that, I'm forgiven.

Who is this woman? She's unlike anyone I've ever
met before. I should stay out of her way, but I *enjoy*
being with her.

And let's not forget that she's the sexiest thing on
two legs. I can't say the petite type has ever turned my
head before. I usually go for curvier women, but some-

thing about Jordan has every nerve ending in my body standing up to take notice.

"Oh, look what I found," she says as she hustles over to a grocery bag sitting in front of the fireplace. She whips out two stockings. "They have our names on them!"

I blink at the oversized socks. Sure enough, *Jordan* and *Nick* are embroidered in red. They're both red with green at the top. Hers has a reindeer on the front, and mine has a Santa.

They're ridiculous.

And kind of cute.

"You hate it," she says. Her expression falls, and she stares down at my stocking. "I think they'll look so cute on the mantel."

"I don't hate it," I reply. I don't want to be a jerk anymore today. If this ridiculous shite makes her happy, then I should let her have it.

It's no skin off my nose.

But if she wants to blare Mariah Carey every day, we're going to have a conversation.

"I'll start dinner after I finish decorating the tree," she says.

"Actually, why don't you take the night off?"

She glances at me in surprise.

"At the store the other day, your cousin asked you to have drinks. You should go do that."

"I'm working," Jordan replies.

"And I'm giving you the night off."

She laughs. "You just said *yesterday* that I work for Nina. Not you. So, you can't give me the night off."

"Take it anyway," I reply and reach out to brush my finger over a loose curl by her ear. "Liam's in town, and he's coming by tonight for pizza and football. You probably don't want to hang out for that."

She wrinkles her nose, and I want to kiss it.

But I don't.

"Yeah, no. That doesn't sound like fun to me. If you're sure?"

"I'm sure."

"Well, okay. But if you need anything, I won't be far. Sid lives in one of the condos less than a mile from here."

"I won't need anything," I reply. "Have fun."

But not too much fun.

Not that it's any of my business. I've kissed her once. It's not like I have a claim to her. The fact that the thought of another man putting his hands on her makes me homicidal is purely my problem.

She grins and reaches for her phone, tapping the screen, then turns back to the tree. "I can't leave without finishing these ornaments. It would drive me nuts to leave it half done."

Her phone lights up, catching her attention.

"Looks like I'm on with Sidney in a couple of hours. I feel like I'm playing hooky."

"You're not," I reply. "Have fun."

She grins, and it's a shot to my heart. This woman has cast some kind of spell on me. "Thanks."

"I'll see you later."

I walk out of the room before I do something monumentally stupid like strip her bare and take her right there on the living room floor in front of the fireplace.

She didn't turn me away yesterday. But she was confused, and I won't make another move unless she makes it crystal clear that it's what she wants.

It'll be good to have her out of the house for a few hours. It'll be great to see Liam and unwind.

"IT SHOULD HAVE BEEN ME," Liam says before taking a massive bite of his pizza.

"Pretty sure your wife would be damn pissed if you took a bullet," I reply.

Liam was the head of security at the royal Montana estate. Until Ellie came and spent time here early last summer, and the two fell hard and fast for each other. Now, Liam's a prince, and Randall took over Liam's old job.

"It hasn't been easy," Liam admits.

"What hasn't?"

"Adjusting. Going from what we do to having other duties. I work closely with law enforcement in London now, and there are jobs I can do, but it's not quite the same."

"Do you regret it?"

"Not for a second," he says and snatches up another slice. "Ellie's the best thing that ever happened to me. I don't know what I'd do without her. I'd be a miserable pain in the ass, that's for sure."

"Sometimes, you still are."

He laughs. "Yeah, well. I don't regret her. I just miss the job at times. And the way it all went down last month left a bad taste in my mouth."

"My shoulder isn't super happy about it either," I reply. "But it's healing, and we'll be back to normal soon enough."

"Yeah, I'm sure you're perfectly content being here with a babysitter, rather than where you're supposed to be."

"Fuck, no. I want to get back to work. But I can't change any of it."

"Good point." He looks up at the screen. We have the game on but muted so we can talk. "Is the job still what you want?"

"What kind of question is that?"

"After the injury, and given some of the shit we saw this summer, are you still content?"

"Yeah, it's what I want. It's what I *know*. And I'm fucking good at my job. Nina's safest when she's with me."

"There's no doubt about that," Liam agrees. "I'm just

checking in. It's not an easy gig. Not everyone is cut out for it."

"There's nothing else I'm cut out *for*."

"Tell me about the girl. I passed her in the driveway. She's a little thing."

"She's a tiny bulldog," I mutter. "She may be small, but she doesn't put up with much, and she's damn strong."

"Have to admire that," he says. "And she'd have to be strong to put up with you."

I smirk. "Yeah, well, she put me in my place today. I've been a surly prick, and she told me to pull my head out of my arse"

"I like her already." Liam laughs. "Anything else going on there?"

"Not yet."

"Interesting choice of words."

"She's great," I admit. "And I'm not usually one to mix business with pleasure. But I like her."

Liam nods. "I'm glad. It would suck if she grated on your nerves."

"Well, she does that, too," I reply, thinking back to the Mariah Carey concert earlier. "But she's here for a while. She's having drinks with her cousin tonight."

"Needed a break, did you?"

"Yeah, actually. Because I *like* her, and I'm not going to push myself on her."

"So, you chose to hang out with me." He presses his hand to his heart. "Aw. I'm touched."

"I'm rethinking that decision."

Liam laughs again and tosses his crust back into the pizza box. "You missed me when I was gone."

"Maybe. There have been lots of new faces lately. How long are you two staying?"

"Until after New Year's. Then, we'll head back with Sebastian and Nina. And, hopefully, you."

"From your mouth to God's ears, my friend."

CHAPTER 5

~JORDAN~

"*E*xtra salt on mine," I say as Sidney lines the rim of a glass for our margaritas.

"How do people drink 'ritas without salt?" she asks as she follows suit with a second glass and then holds them out for me to fill.

I pour the blended goodness into our glasses, add a straw to each, and then Sidney leads me to her living room. She sits on her couch, and I curl up in a chair across from her, sipping my tart drink.

"These are seriously delicious."

She smiles and dips a chip into the guacamole.

I frown at the little designer handbag sitting on her coffee table. "What, exactly, do you use that for? It's not big enough to actually be a purse."

"It's a clutch," she says around another chip. "A conversation piece. And it's big enough for a credit card, a bit of cash, and some lipstick."

"And a condom," I add with a sly smile. "Don't forget that."

Sidney giggles and sips her margarita. "It'll totally hold a condom. Not that I need one lately. Boys are dumb."

"Totally dumb."

My lips are starting to tingle, and I'm only halfway through my first drink.

I'm a lightweight.

"Speaking of idiot boys, tell me about Jeremy."

I scowl into my tequila concoction. I was diplomatic when I spoke about my ex-boyfriend to Nick. I don't have to be quite so nice with Sidney.

"Well, it turns out, he's a dick."

She smirks. "Honey, Jeremy was always a dick, going all the way back to high school."

"But he wasn't a dick to *me*," I reply. "It was a bad couple of years. He got more and more controlling."

I tell her about the last big blowup, where he smacked me across the face, sending me into the dining room wall.

"Motherfucker. I'll take his balls off the next time I see him," Sidney says.

"Anyway, I honestly don't care about him. I saw him at the gym the other day and felt *nothing*. I don't even feel sorry for him. I mean, I don't wish bad things on him, but I just don't care."

"Why would you? He's a dick." She walks into the kitchen and retrieves the pitcher of margaritas and refills our glasses. "Okay, enough about him. He's ruining this pleasant buzz I have going."

"Me, too."

She plops back onto the couch, and her black cat, Luna, jumps onto the arm of the sofa next to her, eyeing me suspiciously.

"I feel like your cat is judging me."

"Yeah, she judges everyone." Sidney reaches out to scratch the feline behind her ears. "Don't you, baby?"

And, just like that, Luna jumps down, flicks her tail, and saunters away.

"She's a diva," Sidney says with a shrug. "Now, tell me the juicy news."

"I have juicy news?" My lips are all the way numb now, and I'm floating on a delightful buzz. "These drinks are potent. And delicious."

"We'll keep making more," Sidney says and passes me the basket of chips. "And yes, you have news. Who is this Nick? And why didn't I know about him before?"

"Ah. Nick." Just the sound of his name has my blood warming in my veins.

Or maybe that's the alcohol.

"He's a hottie," Sid says.

"Right? Like, why does he look like that? He must have hit the genetic jackpot. He's kind of my client."

I explain how I know him, and then cover my mouth with my hand and stare at my cousin in horror.

"You can't repeat that. It's confidential."

"I'm not going to tell anyone," she says. "So, does this mean you can't have sex with him?"

"I don't know. He kissed me." I shove a chip into my mouth. "And I liked it."

"Yeah, I can see where that wouldn't suck, Jordan."

I giggle and sip my drink. "I would kiss him again. He's hot. He's also *very* grouchy."

"That's not hot."

"But then I called him out on it, and he got better."

"Did he apologize?"

"Yeah."

"Okay, that's progress. You should do him. He can be your rebound sex since the odds are you won't marry him."

I blink at her. At both of her. "Why can't I marry him?"

"I don't know. I mean, you probably could. If you want to. Do you want to? Jesus, we've had too much to drink."

"I don't know if I want to marry him. He doesn't like Christmas."

"Is he a Nazi?"

I grin at her. "I don't think so. Maybe he had a tragic childhood where his parents died in a fire, and he lived the rest of his life in an orphanage with no Christmas presents."

"Oh my God, did he tell you that?"

"No, I'm just guessing."

"You're so dramatic when you drink," Sid says. "You

could probably talk him into liking Christmas a little bit. What else do we know?"

"Not a lot," I admit, and I don't like that realization. "I'm going to get to know him better. He's my patient, after all."

"And you can get to know him while you're naked."

"Yes. No. Wait."

Sidney dissolves into laughter. "This is going to be fun."

I yawn. "I should probably head back. But I can't drive."

"I can't drive either."

I nod, thinking it over. "It's not that cold out. I can walk. The snow is nice."

"Take my flashlight with you," she says, gesturing to the end table with a drawer. "It's in there. The bears are sleeping, so you should be safe."

"That's what I was thinking."

Sidney's stretched out on her couch, and she's falling asleep when I take our glasses and the last of the chips into the kitchen. I shrug into my coat and lean over to kiss her cheek.

"I missed you."

"Mm-hmm," she says. "Be careful."

I let myself out of her condo and take a deep breath. The cold air feels so good. It doesn't even feel too frigid. It snowed all day today, leaving about six new inches of powder on the ground, but the sky is clear now and full of stars.

I'd walk on the sidewalk, but it hasn't been plowed. Neither has the street, actually, but I can walk in the tire ruts.

I wore my big, puffy jacket over to Sid's, and as I walk, I feel warm, so I unzip it and let the air flow around me. I can't feel my toes anyway, and my nose starts to drip just a bit.

But it feels fantastic.

I love Montana.

I love Sidney.

And I love margaritas.

The air around me is hushed from the snow and well-lit from the moon. It's an easy walk to the lake house where the sexy-as-all-get-out Nick is.

I want to jump his bones. Bad. Like, I just want to strip myself naked and tell him to come 'n' get it. Which is so *not* like me. I've only ever been with Jeremy, and that wasn't really anything fantastic or worth writing home about.

But I think Sidney's right. I could totally have sex with Nick. He could be my rebound. It sounds fun.

I walk up the driveway and see that only Nick's car is here. I have no idea what time it is.

I try to open the door but then remember that my keys are in my purse.

And my purse is still at Sidney's condo.

"Damn it," I mutter and ring the doorbell. It's like deja vu from the day I first arrived.

Nick pulls open the door and frowns down at me.

"Oh, my God. Are you okay? Did your car break down?"

"No. I walked. Because I'm drunk."

He blinks, and then his frown turns into a scowl. "You *walked*?"

"Sure. It's not far."

"It's the middle of the fucking night," he says and then takes me in from head to toe. "And you don't have boots, gloves, or a hat."

"Nope. Isn't it great? It felt so good. And you're killing my buzz, so let me inside."

He steps back, and I walk past him.

"I have to remember to call Sid tomorrow. I forgot my purse there. She has a condom purse."

"A what?"

"A purse that's only big enough for condoms. Because, you know, a girl has to be prepared for anything. Do you have condoms?"

I let my coat slide down my arms and land in a heap on the floor. Before I can bend over to get it, Nick does it for me, and his hand brushes mine.

"You're fucking freezing. Come on."

He leads me into the living room in front of the fireplace.

"Do you?" I ask again.

"Do I what?"

"Have condoms."

He shakes his head. "I think so, yeah. Do you need some?"

"Maybe, if things go well. It's good to be prepared, you know?"

"So you said." His jaw clenches. Maybe the thought of having sex with me isn't a good one. It seems to have made him grumpier.

"Why are you grouchy again?"

"Because you walked home in the middle of the damn night. If you needed a ride, you should have called me."

"I don't have your number," I say, realizing that for the first time.

"Give me your phone."

"Bossy," I mutter as I take my cell out of my pocket. After it's unlocked, I pass it over. He taps the screen a few times and then hands it back. "Now I have your number. But I was perfectly safe."

"You were alone after midnight."

"Yeah, in Cunningham Falls, Montana, Nick. What did you think would happen? The bears are asleep."

"Just call me next time."

"I don't do this often," I say with a sigh. "And you might have totally killed my buzz. It was so nice. I don't remember the last time I had drinks with Sid. Also? Her cat is a judgy bitch."

He raises a brow.

"I mean, all I did was drink margaritas and talk about having sex with you."

Both brows raise.

"We haven't had sex."

I sigh. "I know. It's sad. But it's okay. I guess the thought of having sex with me makes you grouchy, because all I did was mention condoms, and you looked like you wanted to punch someone."

"Only because I thought you wanted to use the condoms with someone else."

I blink at him. "Who?"

"I have no idea."

"Me either. So, it's not a bad idea?"

"Oh, it's probably a colossally terrible idea," he says with a laugh. "But I'm having a hard time keeping my hands to myself."

"You're actually doing a very good job of it. You haven't touched me much. Is it because I'm a pressional?"

"A what?"

"A pressional. You know, a nurse."

"A professional?"

"That's what I said."

He laughs, his shoulders relax, and his eyes warm up. "No. That's not why."

"Oh. Why, then?"

"Because I'm not going to sexually harass you."

I frown. "I don't feel harassed."

"Good." He takes my hands and pulls me to my feet. "On a scale of one to ten, how drunk are you?"

"I'd say I'm still solidly around a five."

"Damn." He sighs, his eyes are on my lips. "Because

when I take you, it won't be when you don't have all your wits about you."

"You're an honorable guy."

His lips twitch. "It's a damn shame."

"Nah, it's good. Because if you were a dick, I wouldn't be thinking about taking all of my clothes off right now."

"Fucking hell," he whispers and clenches his eyes shut. "You'd tempt the pope."

"He's too old for me." I press in closer, wanting to feel the heat of him. I want him naked, and I want him to do things to me.

Sexy things.

But it's not going to happen tonight.

"Nick?"

"Yes."

"I think I might throw up."

CHAPTER 6

~NICK~

*S*he presses her hand over her mouth and
takes a deep breath.

"Whoa, easy there." I rub big circles over her back,
but she stands like she's going to make a run for it, so I
pull her into my arms and continue rubbing her back
as I kiss the top of her head. "Just breathe, sweetheart.
In through the nose, out through the mouth. Nice and
easy."

She does as I say, several times, and then lets out a
long sigh.

"Okay. I think it's over."

"Did you have a nice time tonight?" I push aside the
thought of her talking about sex and taking all of her
clothes off. Those thoughts will only lead to an uncomfortable night because she's in no shape for sex.

"Yeah." Her voice is small against my chest. "It was
fun. Even the walk home."

That's something we'll talk about again tomorrow. I don't care if we are in the middle of a safe, rural town, I don't want her walking alone, especially late at night.

"Let's get you into bed."

She looks up at me with tired eyes. "I can't do the sex tonight. I thought I could, but I'm tired. And not sexy."

"I always think you're sexy." I lift her easily into my arms, pleased when my injured shoulder doesn't sing in pain. She's a tiny little thing. Jordan presses her face to my neck as I climb the stairs and walk down the hall to her bedroom. I set her on the bed and turn to the dresser to snag some kind of nightshirt. "Can you change by yourself?"

She blinks her eyes open. "Sure."

"Good." I pass her the shirt and walk into the bathroom, where I make myself useful by wetting a washcloth. I take my time, wanting to make sure Jordan's changed by the time I return to her room.

It's just my luck that she's bent over the bed, pulling the covers back. She's in her little red T-shirt and black knickers, and I have a perfect view of her arse.

My dick gives zero fucks that we aren't having sex tonight.

I close my eyes and think of spaghetti. My grandmother. The London Eye.

And when I open them again, Jordan's in bed, frowning at me.

"What are you doing?"

"Meditating," I reply. It's not a lie. I cross to her, sit near her hip, and press the cold cloth to her forehead.

"Oh, that's nice."

"It should help with the nausea."

"I never knew this trick, and I'm a nurse." She swallows hard. "You shouldn't have carried me up the stairs."

"Why?"

"Because you have an *injured shoulder.* That's the whole reason I'm here, to keep you from doing things like that. It was totally irresponsible of me."

"My shoulder did just fine."

Her eyes are closed, but her legs are restless, moving under the covers.

"Are you hurting?" I ask.

"No, I like the way the cool sheets feel against my skin."

I want to climb in there with her. I want to hold her close and protect her.

And if I'm being brutally honest with myself, that scares the ever-loving shite out of me.

I hardly know this woman. I want to know more. I want to learn more. I'm drawn to her, and I don't understand why, but I'm not willing to stop now.

She looks so small, so beautiful against the white sheets in the moonlight.

I refold the cloth and press the cold side against her skin.

"I don't like to be too hot," she continues. "Arizona is too hot."

"Get some sleep, beautiful girl."

Her eyes open and find mine. "You're a nice person, Nick. Sometimes, you're grumpy. But mostly, you're genuinely nice, and I think that's way sexier than your muscles for days."

I feel my lips twitch in response. "I think that's the alcohol talking."

She just smiles and closes her eyes again. I lean over to press my lips to her forehead. By the time I leave the room, she's breathing deeply and evenly.

I jog down the stairs to the kitchen, grab a beer, and then walk into the living room to stare into the fire.

I've always put the job first. Since I was a child, it's been the only constant in my life—and my biggest passion. I'm still looking forward to getting back to my position.

But for the first time in my life, something has distracted me. That makes me think maybe there's something more for me than work. Liam made it work. Yes, he had to leave the job, but I wouldn't be with a princess. Other guards that work for the royal family have spouses and children.

Children.

I drain the rest of my beer and drag my hand through my hair.

Christ. I need sleep.

~

THE NOISE COMING from downstairs is loud and constant. I roll over, the sheets tangling around my hips as I check the time.

Nine.

I don't remember the last time I slept this late. Usually, I only catch a couple of hours at a time. It's a force of habit and a consequence of the job.

I push to the side of the bed and reach for my jeans. I pull them up over my bare hips and, without fastening them, walk over to the closet to find a shirt.

After I use the facilities, I go to investigate the sounds coming from down below. I stop at the entrance to the kitchen and watch in fascination as Jordan pulls a sheet of cookies out of the oven and sets them on a wire rack to cool. The entire kitchen is covered in bowls and pans, flour, and eggs.

It looks like a bakery exploded.

"Good morning," Jordan says with a big smile. "I hope I didn't wake you. I didn't turn any music on or anything, even though I normally would while I bake. But I figured you must be really tired because we were up so late last night."

"I don't usually sleep much," I admit as I sit on a stool and watch her bustle about. It smells good in here.

"I made you muffins for breakfast," she says and reaches for a platter. "Huckleberry. As a thanks for last night. You really shouldn't have carried me, by the way. But I appreciate you being so nice."

"Did you expect me to let you fend for yourself?"

"Oh, that's what I'm used to," she says. There's no censure in her voice, it's just a simple statement of fact.

It makes me want to punch the bloody wall.

"Oh, and here, I'm making you some coffee to go with your muffins."

She hustles over to the single-cup coffee maker and pops in a pod. When it's finished brewing, she pours just the right amount of cream in and passes it to me.

"Why are you looking at me like that?" she asks with a laugh.

"Are you the same woman who was pissed last night?"

"Yeah." She cringes. "Sorry."

"How are you not hungover?"

"I never get hungover," she says and wrinkles her nose. "I know, it's not fair. I also don't drink much, so just a couple of drinks make me completely tipsy. It's ridiculous. I'm a cheap date, *and* I feel great the next morning."

I bite into a muffin and almost fall out of my chair. This might be the best thing I've ever put in my mouth.

Until I taste her.

"Well? What do you think?"

"I think I'll be eating this whole platter."

She laughs and goes to work rolling out cookie dough.

"That's okay. I have more set aside for tomorrow. Do you have plans today?"

I sip my coffee and watch her move about the kitchen. Her movements are concise. Sure. When she reaches above her head for another bowl, I catch a glimpse of pale skin at her stomach, and it's almost enough to bring me to my knees.

"Nick?"

"Yes?"

"Do you have plans?"

"No."

"Good. You can help me decorate all of these cookies. Then we'll take them and deliver them to people."

"Why?"

She frowns. "Because it's fun."

I reach for another muffin.

"Haven't you ever made Christmas cookies before?"

"No."

"Never?"

"Never."

She wiggles a cookie cutter in flour and then pauses, looking at me. "Did your parents die in a fire, leaving you to be raised in an orphanage?"

I bark out a laugh of surprise. "No."

"Good."

"My parents died in a car accident when I was a boy. I was raised by my grandmother."

Her face pales. "Shit. I'm sorry."

"Don't be."

"Your grandmother didn't believe in Christmas?"

"She worked long hours. She's a good woman. And she did what she could. But I can't say that holidays were at the top of her priority list."

"I think that's sad."

"I don't."

I pop the last of the muffin into my mouth and lean back, watching her. "Listen, there's no need to feel sorry for me. I had a good childhood, and then I went into the military. Special Forces. After I got out, I started working for the royal family. I'm able to help my grandmother, and I like my job very much."

"Well, that's good."

"And what about you?"

She starts cutting shapes into the cookie dough. "What about me?"

"Tell me about your family."

"Oh. Sure. Well, my dad died when I was twelve—massive heart attack at forty-five. It was completely out of the blue. So, it's only been my mom and me for a long time. No siblings. I do have a lot of cousins, as I mentioned, and a huge network of people in this community. My family has been in Cunningham Falls for generations."

"So you know Liam Cunningham?"

"I know his family, but I've never met him. Didn't he just marry the princess?"

"Earlier this year," I confirm.

"It's a small world," Jordan says. "And now you need

to come over here and *help me*. I'm not going to do all the work and let you take the credit when we deliver these."

"I think watching is safest."

"No way." She comes around the island, takes my hand, and drags me back around with her. "Come on. You're not afraid of some hard work, are you?"

SHE WASN'T KIDDING. We spent all day baking and decorating, and when it was time to run around town with our goods, I was covered in flour and sugar and tired. But it was fun to see the reactions when we surprised people with the cookies. We even took a big box to the royal house and delivered some to Sebastian, Nina, Ellie, and Liam, then more down at HQ.

Jordan was bubbly and happy and made sure to tell everyone that I helped her.

Liam will never let me live it down.

But now, we're back at the little lake house, sitting with a pizza by the fire.

"Oh my God, this tastes so good," she says. "Ciao makes some damn good pizza."

"I'm exhausted," I admit, and Jordan narrows her eyes at me.

"You overdid it. Is your shoulder hurting?"

"No, all of me hurts." I laugh and shift in my chair.

"How is it possible that I work my ass off and feel fine, but one day of baking has me aching?"

"Because you're not used to it," she says. "Totally normal. You need a hot shower."

"How do you feel?"

"Tired, but good. It was fun to deliver the cookies today. I had a good time. You did a great job, by the way."

"Oh, I think it was pretty obvious which ones I decorated, and which ones were yours. But I tried."

"You didn't do too bad for a newbie."

"You're always so upbeat. Happy."

"Being sad is a waste of time," she says with a shrug. She takes a bite of her pizza. Sauce lingers at the corner of her mouth. Before she can lick it away, I reach out, swipe at it with my finger, and then lick it off. Her eyes dilate.

My dick stiffens.

"Jordan, if you don't want me to kiss you, you'd better say so now."

She sets her plate aside, and I drop my slice back into the box.

She straddles my lap, wraps her arms around my neck, and plants those gorgeous, plump lips on mine.

Mind. Blown.

CHAPTER 7

~JORDAN~

"*D*efinitely." I kiss his chin. "Want you." Kiss his nose. "To kiss me."

His arms wrap around me, and those big hands of his glide up my back to my shoulders and then down to my hips. I've been watching him all day, been two feet from him in the kitchen where we laughed and talked and *enjoyed*. For the first time, I feel like I've spent time with the *real* Nick, not the wounded bodyguard.

And I'm done keeping my hands to myself. If the injured man is sexy, this happy, jovial man is absolutely irresistible.

I'm careful not to grab onto his injured shoulder, but aside from that, I attack him with gusto. I've been waiting for days for Nick to kiss me again. And I may have been impaired last night, but I remember the chemistry between us, and his admission that he's open to this.

Thank goodness.

"You're going to make me crazy," he mutters against my lips as he slows the kiss. "We're not in a hurry, sweetheart."

I press myself against his jean-clad crotch and watch his eyes dilate, making me grin.

"I'm not rushing, I *want you.*"

He growls deep in his throat, and it only turns me on more. He easily stands with me in his arms, and I pull back to scowl at him.

"Stop lifting me. I'm here to make sure you don't hurt yourself."

"I'm not hurting," he says as he lays me gracefully on the floor in front of the fireplace. "Trust me, I'm not daft. I won't do anything to injure myself further."

"Have I mentioned that I love your accent?" I ask as he tugs my sweater up my stomach and presses his talented lips to the skin just above my navel.

"I don't believe so."

"Well, I do. It's not super thick, but it's there." He unfastens my jeans and manages to wiggle them down my legs and then tosses them aside. The warmth from the fire surrounds me. I sigh as Nick peppers my skin with open-mouthed kisses, moving from the inside of my knee to just below the promised land.

"Oh my," I breathe and bury my fingers in his thick, dark hair. Suddenly, I can't say anything at all as he hooks his finger in my panties and moves them out of his way.

He's not rough. In fact, his touch couldn't be gentler as he glides his fingertip through my folds.

"I'm monumentally pissed at myself," he mutters.

"Why?" My hips arch as he pushes just a bit farther inside.

"Because you've been here all this time, and *this* was waiting for me."

Without another word, he leans in and feasts. That's the only word I can use for what he does. He's going to town down there like it's his damn job.

And God bless him for it.

I'm still in my sweater, nearly naked from the waist down, and the sexiest man I've ever met in my life is making a meal out of me.

I mean, am I the luckiest girl in the world, or what?

My legs start to shake. My spine tingles. I'm pretty sure I just went blind.

And then I break completely apart.

Nick kisses up my stomach and tugs my sweater over my head. When he's settled over me, resting on his elbows, he grins down at me.

We're on the living room floor.

And I just had the best orgasm of my freaking existence.

"How are you, sweet girl?"

"Oh, you know." I blow out a breath and stare at his lips. "Average."

He narrows his eyes. "Average?"

I giggle and drag my fingertips up and down his biceps. "Is this hurting your shoulder?"

"Fuck my shoulder."

"I'd rather fuck something else, but only if your shoulder doesn't hurt."

His lips twitch, and he leans in to nip the corner of my mouth. "I like your sass."

And with that, he kisses me like a man starved. He wiggles out of his pants and helps me out of my bra and panties. I hear the sound of a packet being ripped, and then he takes one of my hands in his, threads our fingers, and pins my wrist over my head.

He glances down between us and nudges his way inside.

I bite my lip.

His eyes fly to mine.

"Okay?"

I nod and sigh when he slowly slides in until he's completely seated, and then growls low in his throat.

"Bloody hell," he mutters.

I lift my legs higher on his hips and invite him to *move.*

"Jordan."

"Yeah?"

"You usually talk nonstop, and now is when you don't? Talk to me. Are you okay?"

"I'm not sure I've ever been better," I whisper and gasp when he starts to move. "Holy shit, Nick."

"God, you're sweet. And so damn tight, I won't last long."

I can't help myself. I bear down on him and watch in fascination as his jaw clenches, and his eyes slam shut. He buries his fingers in my hair and makes a fist, pulling the strands and tugging enough to hurt, but only a little.

It's freaking amazing.

"Jordan," he says, just before every muscle in his body contracts, and he falls over the edge of his orgasm.

Nick is the most amazing man I've ever met.

And as cliché as it sounds, I might have just fallen in love with him.

"Why are we going to this again?" Nick asks the following afternoon as I wrap my scarf around my neck.

"Because it's the Christmas Stroll," I say and watch as he zips up his puffy Northface coat. Even in that puffy jacket, his body is off the rails.

How is he legal?

"And?"

"And it's tradition. Besides, I haven't gone in a long time. I'm finally back in town, and I'm not missing it. Besides, you'll like it."

"How do you know that?"

"Because it's the *Christmas Stroll*." I roll my eyes and open the door, shooing him outside to the car. "It's not too cold outside, and there are all kinds of vendors. We'll wander around Main Street, do a bit of shopping, some eating. You know, be members of the community."

He nods and slips into the car beside me.

"Whatever you say."

"Honestly, if you don't want to go, you don't have to."

I haven't started the car yet. I don't want him to feel like I'm making him go anywhere. I'd rather go with him, but if it sounds horrible to him, I shouldn't push it.

"I'm all yours, sweetheart."

I start the car and grin at him. I know he means just for tonight. He's all mine *tonight.* And at some point in the near future, this will all be over, but I'm determined to enjoy him while I have him.

The sex last night? Ridiculous. I didn't know people could have sex like that, and so many times in one evening. My experience has always been once, in the dark, under the covers.

I don't think Nick and I did it even once in the dark last night.

I stop at a light and think about it.

Wait! Yes, we did. When Nick woke me up at like two in the morning.

I had no idea sleepy sex was so...sexy.

"What are you smiling about?" he asks and reaches over to hold my hand. He brings my fingers up to his lips for a kiss.

"Nothing."

"That smile is absolutely not about nothing."

I clear my throat and drive when the light turns green. "I might have been thinking about two in the morning."

He blinks, and then a slow smile spreads over his handsome-as-hell face.

"Were you now?"

"Maybe."

He kisses my hand again.

"It seems I'm having a hard time keeping my hands off you now that I've had you. Seen every inch of you. Been inside you."

"Do you want me to wreck this car?"

He laughs and shakes his head. "No. I'm just being honest. But I'd better stop if I plan on walking through Cunningham Falls without an erection."

"I mean, that could be a conversation starter, but it's probably for the best if you don't."

He takes a deep breath. "Agreed. Okay, so who will we see here?"

"Most people come to this unless they're sick or working. I'd like to stop in and see my cousin Willa at Dress It Up. She owns that clothing store, and she always has a big to-do during the stroll. And then we'll just see people as we walk along." I bite my lip as something occurs to me. "Though I should warn you."

"That sounds ominous."

"We might see my mom."

I park behind Willa's shop. Parking around town is tough on nights like tonight, and it pays to have family who own businesses.

"You haven't talked much about her."

I cut the engine but don't make a move to get out of the car yet.

"It's not that I don't love her. I do. But she gets on my nerves like no one else in the world. She's bossy and demanding, and she can hand out a guilt trip like it's candy on Halloween."

"Good to know."

"Okay, then." I slip my beanie over my head and my hands into my mittens, and we're off. "Let's start at Dress It Up since we're right here."

"I'm with you," he says, but his eyes are already scanning the area. "Wherever you want to go."

"Are you ever able to turn the bodyguard off?" I ask casually.

"What do you mean?"

"You're already scanning the people around us. Your body is stiff. You're on high alert. And I'm not saying that's a bad thing, I'm just wondering if you're ever able to let yourself relax and be a man."

"I'm both," he says after thinking it over for a few

moments. "I'm a man *and* a bodyguard. I've been military since I was eighteen. It's part of who I am."

I nod and then smile when I see Willa passing around a tray of champagne.

"Hey, Jordan," she says and leans in to kiss my cheek. "You look amazing, as always. Hi, Nick."

"Willa," he says with a nod.

"That's right, you guys already know each other."

Willa is friends with Nina and hangs out with her often. So, of course, Nick has been around when the ladies got together.

Not to mention, Willa attended all three of the royal weddings.

"How are you feeling?" Willa asks him.

"Much better, thank you. Looks like you're going to be busy this evening."

"That's the goal," she says with a wink. "I hope you have fun tonight. I have some sales going on, but you're always welcome to come and poke around. And, of course, I'll always give you the *sale* price."

"Because you're the best," I reply. "I do need some new jeans and stuff. My ass has grown since I've been home. Christmas cookies, and all that."

"Girl, I wish I had your ass issues," Willa says with a laugh. "I have some cute jeans coming in next week. Come have a look."

"I will. See you later."

We walk away, leaving Willa to her job.

"Your ass hasn't grown," Nick says when we're out of earshot.

"Yes, it has." I sigh in happiness when Nick takes off my mitten and then slips our clasped hands into his coat pocket. "I haven't been running like usual. But it's winter, and that happens. It's no biggie."

"I happen to like your ass," he says. But his eyes are still alert, dancing through the people.

"I like your ass, too," I reply with a laugh. "Do you like hot chocolate?"

"That's a silly question. Of course, I do."

"Let's get some, then. There's a vendor set up just across the street."

We step off the curb into the street that's free of vehicles and open to foot traffic only. We get into position for some hot chocolate. The line moves a little slow because people like to chat.

How's the family?

Do you like your new job?

Did you hear about the new community center being built?

But that's just how it is in small towns. And it doesn't bother me at all.

It doesn't seem to bother Nick either, as we stand silently, taking it all in. Once we have our hot drinks, we walk down the street.

"I admit, there are more people out here than I anticipated," Nick says. "It's cold, and it's dark."

"Yes, but there are little campfires going on each

block, and all of the holiday lights are lit up. There's music. And food. Come on, admit it. It's fun."

"It's fun," he says and smiles down at me. "I'm glad we came."

"Me, too."

"There you are."

I turn and smile at my mom. She's a little woman with features similar to mine.

"Hi, Mom." I lean in and give her a hug. "This is Nick, the patient I was telling you about."

"Oh, hello," she says with a smile.

"Lovely to meet you."

"Oh, you have a British accent. Isn't that fancy?" I roll my eyes, but Mom doesn't see it. "Jordan left me to go live with you, you know."

Nick's gaze moves to mine. "No, I wasn't aware."

"Of course, you're perfectly able to take care of yourself."

"She just got back to town a couple of months ago," she continues as if I didn't say anything at all. "She couldn't get out of the house fast enough. You'd think she doesn't like me or something."

"Or, you know, I'm twenty-five and probably don't want to live with my mother. Not that we need to have this conversation here, especially in front of Nick."

"You're right. Come to dinner this week. We'll talk then."

"I'll call you, Mom."

"You'd better," she says. "Have fun, kids."

She rushes off to join her friends from her book club.

"Told you," I say as we continue on our way. I sip my hot chocolate. "She's impossible."

"She's a mum," he says with a smile. "And she misses you. Have dinner with her. Then she won't give you such a hard time."

I think it over and concede that he's right. "Good point. Okay, I will." Nick stops walking, and I frown up at him.

"One o'clock," he says in a low voice. I follow his gaze and see Jeremy walking straight towards us, his face set in a hard expression, his stride full of purpose.

"Well, damn," I mutter and mentally square my shoulders. "I've got this."

"I have no doubt," Nick says.

"Hey, Jor," Jeremy says. He reaches out to touch me, but I duck away. He scowls. "I'm not going to hurt you."

"I know that. Ever again. What's up?"

"Listen, I just wanted to come over and tell you that I'm happy for you. You've wanted to move home for a long time, and I'm glad to see you did it, and you're moving on with your life." He holds his hands out at his sides. "I'm just trying to do the same."

"Good."

"The thing is, with the court stuff going on, my security clearance is gone. You know I need that for my job, Jordan. I don't mean you any harm. I'm just asking you to drop the charges so I can move on with my life."

I tilt my head to the side, watching him with clear eyes. I respond in a low voice, so all of Cunningham Falls doesn't hear.

"No. I won't be dropping anything, Jeremy. You manipulated and controlled me for a long time, and I put up with it. That's on me. But then you decided to put your hands on me. And I won't stand for that. Maybe some inconvenience with the court, and your job, will teach you a needed lesson about bullying people."

Jeremy's nostrils flare, and his lips flatten.

His hands fist.

But I don't back down. This is an old scare tactic.

"You don't scare me," I add when it appears that he's waiting for me to change my mind.

"You're such a cold, ugly, skinny bitch," he spits out before he steps forward, determined to get in my face.

But Nick is fast and moves between us.

"Before you make another move, you might want to see what kind of audience you have," Nick says in warning.

Jeremy looks over his shoulder to find Brad Hull, the chief of police, standing with his arms crossed over his chest, watching.

"Problem?" Brad asks.

"We're just talking," Jeremy says.

Brad steps forward and gets within inches of Jeremy's face. "I know all about you, Jeremy, remember? I also know there's currently a restraining order against you, and you're violating that. So, unless you want to land your ass in jail and add to those problems you're already having with your job, I'm going to suggest you leave Jordan alone."

"Fucking bitch," Jeremy sputters as he storms off.

"If he so much as sends you a text message," Brad says as he turns to me, "I want to know about it. I think I'll pay him a visit tomorrow and strongly suggest he go back to Arizona. Have a nice evening."

Brad leaves us, and the crowd that stopped to listen disperses.

Nick's a tight ball of energy.

"I'm fine," I say and turn to him. "Hey, look at me."

His eyes meet mine.

"I'm fine," I say again. "And I handled it."

"Doesn't mean I don't still want to beat him bloody," Nick says, but he sighs and takes my hand. "And, yes, you handled yourself beautifully. I'm proud of you for not backing down."

"I don't like bullies," I say with a shrug and do my best to brush it off and enjoy the rest of the evening. "Now, I need some kettle corn and maybe some cotton candy."

"I hate to mention this, for fear of losing my manhood, but didn't you say you've outgrown your pants because of sweets?"

"You heard me," I reply with a smile. "I'm buying new pants. Let's get some extra corn to take home."

CHAPTER 8

*I*t's been a fucking cold week since the night of the stroll. Winter seemed to settle over Cunningham Falls and close a tight, frigid fist around us.

I've been in the cold before, but twenty degrees below zero is just bloody ridiculous.

Thankfully, I've spent the cold days inside with Jordan. We've settled into a routine, and that surprises me almost as much as the fact that I'm quickly learning that the prospect of being without her makes my gut ache.

We have sex in the morning. And not just any sex. No, the best damn sex of my life. I only had to come all the way to Cunningham Falls, Montana, to find it. We share breakfast, and then I don't see her for a few hours as she and I work out separately. She bakes, and I watch from my perch at the island. Sometimes, she twists my arm, and I help, but I prefer to watch her sure, small hands as they knead dough or scoop cookie batter out of a bowl and onto a pan. She's told me stories about her family, about people here in town, and what it was like to grow up here. I've learned that she loves her job and can't wait to finally find a full-time position here.

She's bloody fascinating. She's been through some shite in her short life, and yet she's as happy and optimistic as they come. I don't get tired of her company. I certainly haven't had enough sex with her. I can't keep my bleeding hands off the woman.

Not that she seems to mind. In fact, she initiates as often as I do. I haven't found any areas that make us incompatible.

This is new. Women don't usually hold my interest for this long. In fact, call me a knob, but I can't remember the last time I wanted to spend this much time in the company of a woman I wasn't working for.

There's something different and alluring about Jordan. I can't imagine being without her. And now that my shoulder has healed nicely, and I'm well on the way to recovery, I know our time together is short.

I don't want to think about it.

A week after the winter storm began, and it seems we're easing out of it a bit with slightly warmer temperatures. It's not balmy, but it won't freeze the nose off your face as soon as you step out, either.

"Let's go outside," Jordan suggests, setting her iPad

aside and clapping her hands. "It's not too bad out there. We'll bundle up and have some fun. We could make a snowman."

I raise a brow. God, she's adorable.

"Or we could just go for a walk," she says. "Or, even better, I think there are inner tubes in the garage. They're probably used for pulling behind a boat, but we can sled on them."

"You want to go sledding?"

She never fails to surprise me.

"Heck, yes. That slope down to the shoreline is perfect."

"And leads into the water."

She rolls her eyes. "It's frozen, Nick. We can slide onto the ice. Come on, it'll be fun."

I want to strip that blue sweater off her delectable little body and consume her—

"Unless you're scared."

Well, then. That'll have to wait because she just threw down the gauntlet.

"Scared?"

"You're not, are you? Wait, is your shoulder bothering you? You've been doing so well, but if it's bothering you, we can just stay in."

"The shoulder's fine. I'm at about ninety-five percent."

"So, you're scared, then."

I narrow my eyes and stand, and she watches me with humor written all over her gorgeous face.

"No, sweetheart, I'm not scared."

"Awesome." She jumps up and runs to the mudroom, where she starts to pile on layers. "It's still pretty cold out, but we'll get a few good runs in. The fresh air will feel fabulous."

"And then we'll come inside, and I'll warm you up."

"I was counting on it." She winks and then shoves her feet into snow boots. "You can unwrap me from all this winter garb."

"Gladly."

When we're clad in coats, boots, gloves, and hats, we set off into the garage to find the tubes. Luckily, they haven't lost their air, and we're ready to go.

"Okay," she says as she adjusts her hat. "Have you done this before?"

"No."

She turns those big eyes up to me in surprise. "Never?"

"No. But it looks pretty easy. Sit and slide, right?"

"Yes. But, if you get into trouble, like you're headed for a tree or something, just bail. Jump off. I wish we had a chair lift, but we'll have to hike back up."

"Good exercise."

She grins. "Ready?"

"Sure."

She sits on her tube and sets off down the hill at a leisurely pace. When she reaches the bottom near the shoreline, she smiles up at me.

"Come on down!" she calls out.

Rather than sit, I dive onto the tube on my stomach and sail down the snow-covered slope, ending up just past her where the water has turned to ice.

"I told you it's frozen," she says as she joins me and points to the middle of the lake. "It's not out there. It'll take another month for it to freeze all the way. But these edges are solid."

I examine the lake. I can see where the ice is thin, about thirty yards offshore.

We're safe here.

"Let's go again," she says, already dragging her tube behind her up the hill. When we reach the top, she turns and smiles at me, and my gut clenches.

"You're beautiful, Jordan."

She swallows. "Thanks."

I cup her cheek and lean in to brush my nose across hers. "And you're getting cold."

"Let's go a couple more times. It's not bad."

I touch her lips with mine. Softly. Just teasing her mouth. Her breaths come faster, but it's not because of the hike up the hill.

"I wonder if I'll ever stop wanting you," I whisper aloud. "Maybe you cast some kind of crazy spell on me."

"If I knew sledding would have this effect on you, we would have done it sooner."

I smile against her mouth.

"Let's have a healthy little competition."

"Okay, what are the stakes?"

"Dinner. If I win, you cook."

"I'll order in if you want."

"No, I want you to cook."

"Darling, you'll go hungry."

She laughs and shakes her head. "The one to slide the farthest out onto the ice wins."

I eye her and the ice again. "I don't know."

"It's frozen," she reminds me. "I used to do this all the time when I was a kid. Me first."

She plops right down on the tube and laughs as she slides down the hill, onto the ice. When she stops, she calls out to me, "Your turn!"

I follow suit and come about ten feet short.

"One more round," she says. "If you beat me, we'll have a tiebreaker."

We climb back up again, and I help her adjust her hat. Then she backs up toward the house.

"What are you doing?"

"Getting a running start," she says and takes off running, then jumps onto the tube on her belly and sets off down the hill.

Everything happens in slow motion. I can see that she's going to slide out too far. She's going to fall into the water.

"Roll off!" I yell. "Jordan, roll off, goddamn it!"

I'm already pulling the phone from my coat and running down the hill when, sure enough, she keeps skidding on the ice and goes out so far that she breaks through, splashing into the water with a loud yelp.

And then she's gone.

I want to panic. Jesus Christ, she could die.

Why did I agree to this?

I immediately remember my training and slide into work mode.

"911," dispatch says into my ear.

"Woman fell through the ice on the lake." I give our location and Jordan's name. "We need services *now*."

"I'm sending them," she replies. "Do not go near her, sir. Our guys will be right—"

I hang up and throw my phone aside, running on the ice. I slide down onto my belly as I get close and scoot to her.

Her arms flail in the water. Thank God she's not under the ice.

"I'm here," I call out. "I'm going to get you out."

"Nick," she says before slipping back in.

Jesus, I've never been so terrified in my life—even when I was shot.

I slowly reach her. If I hurry and fuck this up, we'll both end up in the water and die. That won't do either of us any good.

"Take my hand."

She's tired.

"Damn it, Jordan, take my hand. Come on, baby. I've got you."

She reaches up, and I slide her out of the water onto

the ice. I want to stand and cradle her to me, but it's too dangerous here.

I manage to scoot us toward shore. I can hear the sirens in the air. Thank Christ, help is coming.

"Stay awake, sweetheart." When I'm sure we're on solid ice, I pick her up and run with her toward the house. I have to warm her up. It's too fucking cold out here. She'll die of hypothermia.

"So cold," she says, her lips already blue and teeth chattering.

"I know. We're going to warm you up. Do you hear that? Help is coming. I've got you, baby."

As I crest the hill, I see the firetrucks and ambulance pull into the driveway.

"I'm taking her inside," I announce to the crew as they jump out of the vehicles to join me. "She's too cold."

They follow me in, and we immediately start stripping her out of the wet clothes. Her breathing is shallow, her skin turning bluer. I reach for two of the throw blankets on the couch and wrap them around her.

"How long was she in the water?" I glance up to see Sam Waters, a friend of Liam's, beside me.

"Two minutes, maybe three."

He's taking her vitals, his lips set in a grim line. "She's going into shock. We need to get her to the hospital."

"I'm coming with you."

He just nods, and I watch as they quickly strap Jordan to a gurney and wheel her into the ambulance. I jump in with them and hold her hand as we set off for the hospital.

"Come on, baby, you have to wake up. We need you awake."

"So tired," she murmurs and slips into sleep.

"Her blood pressure is dropping," Sam says. "We need to warm her the fuck up."

I strip out of my coat, open my flannel shirt, and join her on the cot, giving her my body heat as Sam places a reflective blanket over us both.

"That'll do until we get to the hospital and get her a heated blanket," Sam murmurs.

"Pulling in now," someone says over the speaker into the back.

We're bustled inside. I refuse to leave the gurney until we're in a room, and nurses come hustling in with heated blankets and physically nudge me aside.

Someone wraps one of the blankets around my shoulders as well, but I ignore it.

She has to be okay.

"Her vitals are looking better," the doctor says as he listens to her breathing. "If you hadn't gotten to her so quickly, things could have been very different."

"Never been so frightened in my life," I mutter and push my hand through my hair, then wince in pain.

"What's wrong?" the doctor asks.

"I had a shoulder injury. I must have wrenched it a

bit when I climbed the hill with her." I shake my head. "I'm fine. Just worry about Jordan."

"We're going to keep her for a few hours and make sure her vitals continue to level out. We'll get some fluids in her and monitor her. You can stay with her if you want."

"Thank you."

I stand back as the nurses start an IV, trade the blankets for fresh, warm ones, and I turn to see Sam standing in the doorway.

"I just wanted to check on her."

"Sam," Jordan says.

We both turn to find her smiling at us.

"It should be illegal to have that much hotness in one room."

Sam smirks. "Stop swimming in winter, okay?"

"Accident," she says, and her eyes droop closed. "Nick saved me."

"What am I, chop suey?" Sam says. He reaches out and rubs her foot. "Call me if you need anything."

"Call my mom, okay?"

"Will do." He turns to me. "Old family friends. It's a small town."

"I'm glad you're here," I reply. "Thank you."

Sam nods. "I'll see you later."

He leaves, and I sit next to Jordan, then take her hand in mine and kiss her cold fingers.

"I know you said you like to be cold, but this is taking things too far," I say.

"Yeah, I'm a drama queen." She smiles up at me. Her skin isn't so blue anymore. Her eyes look tired, but they're clear.

I feel myself breathe for the first time since she took off on that tube.

CHAPTER 9

~JORDAN~

I've never been so cold—or scared—in all my life.

"I think our sledding days are over," Nick says. He's kissing my hand like it's his lifeline. "We'll stick with snowmen."

"I'm okay." I squeeze his hand. "Honest. I'm feeling much better."

"I'm not," he admits and closes his eyes. He has dark circles under them, and he looks as if he's been awake for days. "You took ten years off my life."

"Hey, I really am okay. I'm warming up. We'll be back at the house before you know it."

He leans in and presses his lips to my cheek. "If you ever pull something like that again, I'll spank your arse red."

"Well, that'll warm a girl up. Who knew I was into spanking?"

His lips twitch, but he doesn't smile.

"I've been through a lot of shite," he says. "From watching men die, to fishing royalty out of a lake, to being shot myself."

"I know." I drag my fingers down his cheek, over the stubble there. He hasn't shaved in a few days. "I didn't know I'd go out that far. I'm sorry, Nick."

He sighs deeply, and his shoulders sag.

"Did I hear you say you hurt your shoulder?" I ask. "And don't you dare lie to me."

"It's sore. Ask me how many fucks I give."

"I give fucks, Nick. I'm supposed to keep you from getting hurt. Not *getting* you hurt. Or something like that."

"All that matters is that you're safe," he says and brushes my hair off my face. "Those men saw you mostly naked, so now I have to kill them all."

"I'm in my bra and panties under here," I remind him.

"Mostly naked," he repeats. "What's up with you and Sam?"

I feel my lips twitch. "He was my first kiss. But I was twelve, and he was fourteen, so I don't think it counts. Why, are you jealous?"

I hold my breath. Is he jealous?

"Of course, not," he says. "I was just curious."

"Uh-huh. That's why you want to murder them all for seeing me in my underwear. Curiosity."

Nick laughs and kisses my lips lightly. "Finish warming up so I can take you home."

The way he's smiling at me gives me shivers. He's tender and sweet. And, dare I say...loving?

"Jordan, there's someone out here who wants to see you," the nurse says, poking her head in the door. "His name's Jeremy?"

"Oh." I blink at her and then look up at Nick, who's scowling at the poor woman. "I guess he can come in."

She nods and leaves, and Nick shakes his head.

"He has no business here. I should call Brad."

"Before you do..." Jeremy says as he walks into the room. His eyes are on me, and he looks scared. "I just wanted to come by and apologize. I tried to call but figured you probably don't have your phone on you."

"It's likely at the bottom of the lake," I say, thinking of my phone for the first time. "How did you know I was here?"

"Dad's police scanner," he says. His father used to be a volunteer fireman and never stopped using the scanner. "Scared me."

Nick's hand tightens on mine. It doesn't go unnoticed by Jeremy.

"I'm not here to cause trouble," he says. "In fact, I wanted to come and apologize...for everything."

"I'm not dropping the charges," I say.

"I know," he replies with a grim nod. "I never should have put my hands on you that way, Jordan. You didn't deserve it. And I was a supreme asshole for causing a scene at the stroll."

"Quite," Nick says.

"I won't bother you again. When I heard about the accident on the lake, I just wanted to make sure you were okay. We may be over, but you were the most important part of my life for a long time, and I want you to be amazing."

"Thanks," I say and offer him a smile. "I want you to be amazing, too. Be nice to the next girl."

"I will." He smiles and then ducks out of the room.

"Well, that was unexpected," I say, staring at the closed door.

"Are you all right?"

"Yeah. I'm glad he apologized. Maybe he needed that closure."

"What about you?"

"Oh, I had closure the second he slapped me." I look into Nick's eyes. "Can we blow this popsicle stand?"

"I thought you'd never ask."

"You're staying in bed," Nick says as he clears my dinner plate away. As soon as we got back to the house, he tucked me into his bed—so he could keep a better eye on me, he said—and has been doting on me like crazy.

I admit, it doesn't suck. But it's completely unnecessary.

"Nick, I'm not an invalid."

He bends over so he's nose-to-nose with me. "For once, just do as you're told."

"Yeah, I don't like that either."

He smirks. "It's one evening of rest, sweetheart. Just let me care for you, okay?"

I sigh dramatically. "This is backwards. I'm supposed to be taking care of you."

"I'm just fine."

"Well, so am I."

"Are you always this stubborn?"

I lift a brow. "No, I'm tired this evening, so I'm less stubborn."

"If you're that tired, staying in bed won't be a hardship for you." He winks and leaves the room, taking my empty plate down to the kitchen.

Rather than argue, I reach for my iPad and open it to the book I've been reading. I'm less than a page in when he returns and walks right past me and into the master bath.

I hear the shower start and imagine him stripping down to get under the hot spray of water. I have to admit, I've enjoyed getting to know Nick. He's smart and kind, has a stellar work ethic, and can even be fun. His moodiness doesn't bother me at all.

But his body? Holy mother Mary, his body is the

sexiest thing I've ever seen. It does things to me that might be illegal in some states.

And he's naked right now.

When I hear the water turn off, I call out to him. "Nick? Can you come in here for a sec?"

He comes to the doorway, a towel slung low around his hips, and his eyebrows raised in question. "What's up?"

"Lose the towel."

Water beads on his chest, his arms, and his neck. His dark hair is still wet.

I want to lick him from head to toe.

His eyes narrow. "Why?"

"I wanna see something. Please?"

He lets the towel fall to the floor, and I soak in the sight of him. Hard muscles, defined beautifully under smooth, tanned skin. Abs for days, and a happy trail of hair that leads south to an impressive cock that's growing by the second.

"You're in no shape for this," he says.

Rather than reply, I strip my tank top over my head and toss it to the floor. "I'm in excellent shape for this."

"You fell into a bloody lake today."

I wave him off and rise to my knees, shucking off my underwear. "That was hours ago. I've had medical attention and lots of rest, thanks to you. It's all your fault, by the way."

"That you fell into the lake?"

"No, that's *my* fault. It's your fault that I want to ravage your sexy body. I mean, *look* at you."

His lips twitch. "Like what you see, do you?"

"Oh, yeah. Come here."

He licks his lips and crosses to me. I reach for his cock, but he captures my wrist in his hand as he climbs over me and pins my hand above my head.

"If you touch me, I'll embarrass myself," he growls.

"Why?"

"Because you make it impossible for me to breathe, much less keep a rein on my dick, Jordan. Your touch makes me lose my ever-loving mind."

"Good to know."

He nuzzles my neck. A drop of water falls onto my chest and weaves a wet path between my breasts.

"You're the most beautiful woman I've ever laid eyes on."

I want to smirk. Brush it off. Chalk up those words to an intense situation today and chemistry.

But his eyes are hot as they roam over my face and shoulders.

"Thank you," I whisper.

"I'm going to take this nice and slow," he says. His voice is hushed as he kisses along my jawline.

"I'm not fragile."

"The fuck, you're not," he replies as his free hand slides up my inner thigh. "Ah, you're ready for me."

"More than ready," I agree, opening wider for him. "So ready."

He leans over me and plants his full lips next to my ear as he slowly begins to slip inside.

"Mine," he whispers. "For now, you're mine."

I may be yours forever.

But I can't speak the words aloud. I don't know what's going to happen when all is said and done.

All I can do is enjoy every second with him. Every touch. Every sigh.

He moves faster, but he's still careful. I reach between us and press a fingertip to my clit, and his pupils dilate.

"You're so damn sexy," he growls. "Ah, bloody hell."

He groans as he falls over the edge, succumbing to his orgasm. He grinds the root of his cock against me, and I follow him over in the most all-encompassing orgasm I've ever experienced.

I can't move. My lips might be numb.

"I'll roll off in about a month," he says, making me giggle. "I can't feel my toes."

"I'm glad I'm not the only one."

He raises his head and smiles down at me. "I don't tell you this often enough, but you're wonderful. I hope you know that."

"I do now." I kiss his chin. "And I think you're pretty wonderful, too."

CHAPTER 10

"We have good news," Randall says at our afternoon meeting. It's been a week since the lake incident.

I still have nightmares.

"Nick has been cleared for duty," he says with a nod at me. "He'll be back to work on Monday."

"About damn time," Liam says as he leans back in his chair. He grins at me.

"Why are you here?" I ask, giving him shit. *"Your Highness."*

He just flips me the bird, and I love that things feel more normal.

We wrap up the meeting, and I hang back at HQ with Liam. Sebastian walks through the door and then frowns when he looks around the now-empty room.

"Did I miss it?"

"Yes, sir," I reply.

"Nina insisted on…well, never mind. I've been meaning to ask you, Nick, how is Jordan feeling?"

"She's great," I reply. "Fully recovered."

"Excellent," Sebastian says.

"So, now what?" Liam asks, smiling at me.

"Now what…what?"

Sebastian leans his shoulder against the wall, listening. "If you think we don't know that you've been having an affair with her, you're mistaken."

"I didn't make it a secret," I reply and rub my hand over my mouth in agitation. "And I don't know what happens next."

"Do you like her?" Liam asks.

"I'm fucking in love with her," I growl. I sound grumpy as shit. Jordan would give me hell for it.

"And he sounds happy about it, too," Sebastian says with a laugh.

"It can't work." I shake my head. "It doesn't matter how I feel about her because it's over. I'll move back here, and she'll get on with her life."

"Why?" Liam asks.

"What do you mean, *why*? Because I work here. This is where I *live*."

"No, why can't you be together?"

I stare at him like he's lost his mind. "Because I live the majority of the year in London, remember? Long-distance relationships suck arse, and asking her to be okay with me being overseas most of the time isn't fair."

"So, she moves to London," Liam says.

"Other royal guards have families," Sebastian adds. "You'll move her there and have a life with her. If we're in Montana for an extended period, you can bring her with you. We're not unreasonable."

"She has a life in Montana," I reply. "She's wanted to live here again for a long time. And she's a nurse. As great as all of that sounds, I can't ask her to uproot her life for me. Her ex did that, and she was miserable."

"You aren't her ex," Liam reminds me. "Have you talked about the future at all with her?"

"No. She's packing her things now."

"Does she seem happy about that?" Sebastian asks.

I stop and think. Jordan had been quieter than usual the last couple of days.

"I don't know."

"Communication," Liam says and wraps his knuckles on the table. "Talk to her, man. Ask her what she wants."

"I truly think you can make it work," Sebastian says. "She can work as a nurse for the family, if she would like that. Or, we can transition you to Nina's Montana security, the way Liam was mine before. You're a valuable member of our team, and we want you to be happy."

"Thank you."

He nods and leaves HQ, headed back to the main house.

"What are you going to do?" Liam asks.

"Talk to her." I blow out a breath. "Here's hoping she's still at the lake."

~

"You just caught me," Jordan says as I walk into the house. Her suitcase is sitting at the bottom of the stairs.

"You're leaving already?"

"Well, you've been cleared to go back to work," she says. "So, my job here is done."

And I haven't asked you to stay.

I'm a bloody wanker.

"I think we need to talk, Jordan."

She licks her lips and then dives into her purse, looking for her moisturizer no doubt.

"Oh?"

"I should have said something before this, but honestly, I'm not sure how to make it work."

"How to make what work?" she asks.

"Us."

I have her undivided attention now. She drops her purse to the floor and stares at me with wide eyes. "Us?"

"Us. Listen, I'm a knob. And I don't mean to be. I've loved spending the past few weeks with you, despite the rocky start we had. You're sweet and fun. Kind. You make me laugh, and you've reminded me what it is to truly *live.* I don't want that to be over."

She sighs in relief, and I feel like an even bigger arsehole.

"I figured you were just ready to get on with your life," she says. "And I don't blame you."

"I do, but I want you to be in it."

"Well, we can certainly be friends."

I shake my head. "I'm saying this all wrong. Jordan, I've fallen in love with you."

Her eyes fill with tears. "You have?"

"Absolutely. I think I was in love with you the minute you bought me a stocking with my name on it."

"I knew I could get you to like Christmas," she whispers, making me grin.

"My life is complicated," I continue and take her hand in mine. "I work out of London, and all over the world, really. And you're in Montana. But I think we have options open to us. Whether that looks like you moving to London, or me taking on a permanent position here in Montana, we can make it work. Because I'm not ready for this to end. I can't imagine my life without you, not now that I have you."

She walks into my arms and holds me tightly, her face pressed to my chest.

"Is this a yes hug, or a goodbye hug?" I ask.

"I love you, too," she says. "Even when you're grumpy. I didn't want to leave, but you haven't said a word about anything permanent, and I'll never be that girl who clings just because the sex is really good."

"Let's be honest, the sex is fucking phenomenal."

She laughs and nods. "It really is. But that's not a basis for a relationship."

"You're right." I tip up her chin so I can look into her eyes. "But friendship is. Trust. Loyalty. And you have all of that in me. I want us to keep learning more about each other. I want to *be* with you, Jordan. Because the thought of being without you is pure torture. I'd rather get shot again."

"That won't be necessary." She boosts up onto her toes and kisses my lips. "I'm yours, Nick. I've been yours for what seems like a long time. I was just looking for you."

I wrap my arms around her and kiss her thoroughly, the way a woman should be kissed when she's just confessed her love.

"So, what are we going to do?" I ask.

"Well, right now, you're going to seduce me. And we'll figure the rest out together."

"I like the way you think."

EPILOGUE

~JORDAN~

One Year Later

*I*t's Christmas. My absolute favorite time of year. We're back in Cunningham Falls for the holidays, and I admit, it's good to be here. I *love* London, way more than I ever expected to, but Montana will always be home.

Whenever we come back to the States, Nick and I stay at Nina's house. He didn't give up his full-time position with the royal family. I couldn't ask him to do that, especially considering that I didn't have a job in Montana to tie us here.

I've been working with the royal medical staff and enjoying it very much. I've learned so much, and now that Ellie and Aspen are both pregnant, I'll be their private nurse during their pregnancies.

I couldn't be happier.

I've just hung our stockings on the mantel when Nick walks into the living room.

"Where did you find those?" he asks.

"I stored them at my mom's in January before we left for London. Now, it's tradition."

He's watching me with that intense gaze he gets that tells me something's on his mind. It won't work to try and pry it out of him.

He'll tell me, eventually.

"Is everyone settled at the main house?"

"They are," he says. "And now we're all alone for the rest of the evening."

"Well, that doesn't sound bad at all."

He sits in a chair and snatches me by the hips, tumbling me into his lap.

"Hello there." I kiss his cheek. "You're ridiculously handsome today."

"I'm glad you think so." His face is so serious, it makes me a little nervous.

Shit.

Is he about to break up with me?

"I need to talk to you about something."

I swallow hard. "Okay."

He takes my hand and laces our fingers together, then kisses each finger, one by one.

"Are you breaking up with me?" I blurt.

"What? No." He chuckles and kisses my cheek. "If that were the case, you wouldn't be nestled in my lap, sweetheart."

"Okay. Continue."

He drags his nose up my neck, sending shivers through me.

"Nick?"

"Hmm?"

"Talk."

"Right." He clears his throat. "I love you."

It always catches me off guard, like a shot right to the heart, every time he says those three little words. Even after all this time.

"I love you, too."

"I've wanted to do this for a while, but I thought it was best to wait until we were here, in this place."

He stands and sets me on the chair, and then, to my utter shock, he lowers down to one knee.

"Holy shit."

He takes my hand.

"Jordan, you are the love of my life. I enjoy you, trust you, and can't wait to share every day with you, from today until the day I take my last breath. I need you by my side, always. Will you please do me the honor of becoming my wife?"

I couldn't stop the tears if I tried. And I don't care. Because this man loves me, tears and all.

"Of course." I wrap my arms around his neck and hold on tight. "Of course, I'll marry you. Can it be a holiday wedding? I mean, it's too soon for this year, but if you're okay with a year-long engagement, we can plan it for next year. I don't know if you'll want to get married here or in London, but—"

He presses a finger to my lips, shutting me up.

"I have to do this first," he says and slips the ring onto my finger. "And this."

He kisses me silly. Every time he kisses me like this —which is pretty much every day—I go positively gooey.

I'm a lucky girl.

He leans back and brushes a lock of my hair out of my eyes.

"We'll figure out the rest. Together."

ABOUT THE AUTHOR

Kristen Proby has published close to forty titles, many of which have hit the USA Today, New York Times and Wall Street Journal Bestsellers lists. She continues to self publish, best known for her With Me In Seattle and Boudreaux series, and is also proud to work with William Morrow, a division of HarperCollins, with the Fusion and Romancing Manhattan Series.

Kristen and her husband, John, make their home in her hometown of Whitefish, Montana with their two cats and dog.

facebook.com/booksbykristenproby
instagram.com/kristenproby
bookbub.com/profile/kristen-proby
goodreads.com/kristenproby

NEWSLETTER SIGN UP

I hope you enjoyed reading this story as much as I enjoyed writing it! For upcoming book news, be sure to join my newsletter! I promise I will only send you news-filled mail, and none of the spam. You can sign up here:

https://mailchi.mp/kristenproby.com/ newsletter-sign-up

ALSO BY KRISTEN PROBY:

Other Books by Kristen Proby

The With Me In Seattle Series

Come Away With Me
Under The Mistletoe With Me
Fight With Me
Play With Me
Rock With Me
Safe With Me
Tied With Me
Breathe With Me
Forever With Me
Stay With Me
Indulge With Me
Love With Me

Dance With Me
Dream With Me

Coming in 2020:
You Belong With Me
Imagine With Me
Shine With Me

Check out the full series here: https://www.
kristenprobyauthor.com/with-me-in-seattle

The Big Sky Universe

Love Under the Big Sky
Loving Cara
Seducing Lauren
Falling for Jillian
Saving Grace

The Big Sky
Charming Hannah
Kissing Jenna
Waiting for Willa
Soaring With Fallon

Big Sky Royal
Enchanting Sebastian
Enticing Liam

Coming in 2020:
Taunting Callum

Check out the full Big Sky universe here: https://
www.kristenprobyauthor.com/under-the-big-sky

Bayou Magic

Shadows

Coming in 2020:
Spells

Check out the full series here: https://www.
kristenprobyauthor.com/bayou-magic

The Romancing Manhattan Series

All the Way
All it Takes

Coming in 2020
After All

Check out the full series here: https://www.
kristenprobyauthor.com/romancing-manhattan

The Boudreaux Series

Easy Love
Easy Charm
Easy Melody
Easy Kisses
Easy Magic
Easy Fortune
Easy Nights

Check out the full series here: https://www.
kristenprobyauthor.com/boudreaux

The Fusion Series

Listen to Me
Close to You
Blush for Me
The Beauty of Us
Savor You

Check out the full series here: https://www.
kristenprobyauthor.com/fusion

From 1001 Dark Nights

Easy With You
Easy For Keeps
No Reservations
Tempting Brooke
Wonder With Me

Coming in 2020:
Shine With Me

Kristen Proby's Crossover Collection

Soaring with Fallon, A Big Sky Novel

Wicked Force: A Wicked Horse Vegas/Big Sky
Novella
By Sawyer Bennett

All Stars Fall: A Seaside Pictures/Big Sky Novella
By Rachel Van Dyken

Hold On: A Play On/Big Sky Novella
By Samantha Young

Worth Fighting For: A Warrior Fight Club/Big Sky
Novella
By Laura Kaye

Crazy Imperfect Love: A Dirty Dicks/Big Sky Novella
By K.L. Grayson

Nothing Without You: A Forever Yours/Big Sky
Novella
By Monica Murphy

Check out the entire Crossover Collection here:

https://www.kristenprobyauthor.com/kristen-proby-crossover-collection

Made in the USA
Columbia, SC
28 December 2020

29789840R00074